The Davidson Affair

ff

THE DAVIDSON AFFAIR

Stuart Jackman

faber and faber
LONDON · BOSTON

First published in 1966
by Faber and Faber Limited
3 Queen Square London WC1N 3AU
First published in this edition 1968
Reprinted 1970, 1971, 1973, 1977 and 1985

Printed in Great Britain by
Whitstable Litho Ltd., Whitstable, Kent

ISBN 0 571 08616 0

For
Hubert Cunliffe-Jones
mentor and friend
in gratitude
and in the hope that he will find
a morsel of bread in the sack

If they do not hear Moses and the prophets,
neither will they be convinced
if some one should rise from the dead.

Luke 16. 31.

$$\boxed{\text{I}}$$

(Excerpt from the script of a Special Report telecast at 9.15 p.m. on Monday, April 16th, from the Rome studios of the Imperial Television Corporation (ITC).

Video	*Audio*
CUT to Andrew Patros M/CU	FADE music
	More trouble in the Middle-East.
	Since early yesterday morning reports of a new crisis in Jerusalem have been coming in. There have been a number of incidents and the Governor-General has imposed a dusk-to-dawn curfew on the city.
	For a full report of these new developments in what is rapidly becoming the Empire's main trouble-spot we are taking you over now on the WTA link to the Jerusalem studios where our special correspondent, Cass Tennel, is waiting.
	Come in, Tennel.
CUT to Tennel	BRING music up

2

The Jerusalem studios occupied a good site on the corner
opposite the Jaffa Gate. From the window of Kapper's
office in the WTA suite on the fifth floor you could look
right across the city to the massive bulk of the Temple
and the green shoulder of the Mount of Olives beyond. It
was a magnificent view and they used it as an interlude
picture between programmes on JTV1—the Jerusalem
channel.

It was the setting for my Report that Monday evening.
They did a back-projection of it on to a screen and gave me
a chair and a desk in front. There was a telephone on the
desk and a small bowl of anemones from Galilee. The
phone was Kapper's gimmick; his own particular visual
cliché. He always has one on the set somewhere. He has a
theory that it gives the viewers a sense of being in touch
and adds a note of expectancy to the programme. The
flowers were my contribution. The fact that they came
from the place where Davidson had spent his boyhood
appealed to the romantic in me.

I sat under the bright lights and watched Drewy Patros
on the monitor. He was the head of the News Department
at ITC and did not normally go in front of the cameras for
anything less than the death of a monarch. Thick-set and
swarthy, with a large round head and a crew-cut, he

crouched in the centre of the screen like a spider into whose web an especially juicy fly had just blundered. Reception was excellent that night and his voice came undiluted over the miles, chewing greedily on the gristle of the words. I suppose it was what you would call an interesting voice, masculine and full of character; particularly if, like the viewers, you only heard it on momentous occasions. But to those of us who had to work with him it was irritating and unwelcome, as ominous as a fire-alarm. In our minds it was associated with the organized chaos out of which TV documentaries were born—the inconvenient journeys to unlikely places, the terrible meals gulped down standing at canteen counters, the frenzied struggle to collect enough facts in an impossibly short time and present them, attractively pre-digested, to a hungry public. Patros looked like a spider and he operated like one, letting himself down unexpectedly into the relaxed pattern of our off-duty time and confronting us with a series of full-blown crises.

When I fumbled for the bedside phone in the Heliopolis Palms Hotel at half-past six that Sunday morning and heard his voice at the other end I knew it meant trouble.

And I was in no mood for trouble.

Greg Dekka and I had been down in the desert for two weeks doing a feature on the Bedouin Spring Festival. It was one of the pseudo-cultural jobs that Toplou had been dreaming up ever since he took over Programmes. Toplou was a Greek who had come into TV at the top, straight from a lectureship in the University of Athens. He was a fussy little man with a head full of brains and a puritanical streak as narrow as his shoulders. In his book the function of television was to edify, not to entertain.

We probably needed him at that. We had been deluging the viewers for years with violence and sex, and the indications were that we had about reached saturation point. The odd thing was that Toplou's carefully planned culture-for-the-masses had a disconcerting trick of turning out to be very much the mixture as before, as though everything that came in through the camera lens got itself processed somewhere in among the wires and tubes to appear on the screen highly-spiced and brutal. Like the Bedouin Festival. In scope and intent it was to have been another uplifting chapter in the story of man's conquest of his environment, and to that end Toplou had packed it tight with anthropological and sociological significance. But all we had managed to get on film were several thousand feet of people indulging in some pretty un-inhibited dancing, a decidedly savage sequence shewing part of the fertility rites, and a rather lascivious glimpse of the village slave-market. In fact, the Circus Maximus all over again—nudity and blood—with a touch of Arab squalor and a slightly self-conscious background of date palms.

After a fortnight of that we were glad to go back to Heliopolis and soak the smell of goat out of our pores and sleep in a decent bed again. Not that we had been in a hurry to get to bed. We had done the round of the night-spots first (bowdlerized variations of what we had seen in the desert, but at least the girls were cleaner) luxuriating in the knowledge that we could sleep most of Sunday before flying back to Rome on Monday morning. Patros, however, had other plans for us.

"Get dressed, Cass," he said over the phone. "I'm sending you to Jerusalem."

"Thanks very much. When?"

"Now. This morning. We've laid on a charter for you

14

with Trans-Med. You take-off from Almaza in exactly fifty-three minutes."

In the other bed Greg opened one eye and slowly focused on me. I put my hand over the mouthpiece. "Patros. We're going to Jerusalem."

"You mean—today?"

I nodded.

"Dear God," Greg said, and closed his eye.

In my ear Patros said, "I know it's a bit sudden, Cass, but. . . ."

"Yes," I said pleasantly. "It is, isn't it?"

"I'm sorry, but this is dynamite. The whole shooting-match could go up any minute."

"I can't wait," I said.

Patros spluttered. "Now look here, Cass, if . . ."

"Okay, Drewy. What's the story?"

"Davidson." The way he scraped out the word it sounded like a match being struck. A match to light a fuse.

"What?"

"Jesus Davidson, for God's sake."

"What about him?"

"They hanged him Friday afternoon."

"Did they now? And what d'you want me to do? Lay a wreath?"

"If what's come through on the teleprinter's right he doesn't need flowers. A good square meal more likely."

I frowned and switched the receiver to my other ear. "Must be a bad line, Drewy. I thought you said he was dead."

"Dead and buried."

"Last Friday?"

"Correct."

"And now he's hungry?"

"Get a grip, Cass. I know it doesn't make sense. But it's come through from Kapper himself, and he's nobody's fool."

I agreed with him there. Nick Kapper and I were old friends. We'd been disc-jockeys together in steam-radio before we moved over into television. In the last few years he had made a considerable name for himself on the production side. Slight and tense, with restless hands and eyes, there was an electric quality about him. He gave you the impression of being wired into the circuit of his control console up there above the studio floor in his little sound-proofed box. He was described rather acidly by his rivals as being married to his job. But even they had to admit that the marriage was highly successful. If he had sent Patros a message it would bear looking into. Even one so bizarre as this.

"What exactly does he say, Drewy?"

"Quote: 'Jesus Davidson, executed for treason Friday, reported seen in city early this morning following small earthquake o-four-hundred hours. Several members Jewish Army guard detail in close arrest pending enquiry. Suggest immediate investigation'—unquote."

I thought about this for a minute. Kapper clearly was taking it very seriously.

"You still there, Cass?"

"Yes," I said. "Drewy, who was—or is—Jesus Davidson?"

Patros chuckled. "Good question, Cass. But you'll have to go to Jerusalem to find the answer. All we know here is that he was a small-town artisan—plumber or joiner or something—who got himself tangled up in politics."

"Oh, one of those."

"Precisely. And with the present state of things in the Middle-East it could snowball in twenty-four hours."

16

"Does he have much of a following?"

"Dunno. That's for you to find out. Incidentally, he called himself Messiah."

"And what's that supposed to mean?"

"Sorry, Cass. No time to go into it now. I want you over there smartly. There's a story here, and we're going to scoop it if it kills you."

"Bless you, Drewy," I said. "I love you too."

"I'm holding fifty minutes open for you on the WTA link tomorrow night. Right after the main news."

"You must be joking. With a thing like this I need at least . . ."

"Anything you need, ask Kapper. He's got it all jacked-up. Just let me see you on camera at nine-fifteen tomorrow night, Okay?"

"Now just a minute, Drewy, I. . . ."

"Make it good, boy," Patros said, and hung up.

The miniature Patros on the monitor screen said, "Come in, Tennel." I heard the music swell briefly and fade, saw the floor-manager's hand drop to cue me in, and turned to face the camera.

"Jerusalem tonight", I said, "is a city of rumour and unrest. Although the hotels and rest-camps are still crammed with pilgrims up for the Jewish Festival an ominous quiet broods over the deserted streets—a quiet broken only by the prowling squad cars and the rumbling half-tracks of the Army patrols. . . ."

They had me in medium close-up, leaning forward across the desk with the huge panorama of the city behind me. We had planned this opening shot with some care for it was here that the mood of the programme had to be established.

Originally we had plumped for something blatantly

dramatic—"Can a man come back from the grave? This is the question on everyone's lips here tonight. . . ." But as the frantic hours passed and the script began to take shape I had become dissatisfied with this approach. It demanded the sort of climax that could only be sustained by a decisively negative answer to the question. And the more I learned of Davidson the less prepared I was to go in front of the cameras and give such an answer.

The story we were building was a political one only on the surface. Underneath it was religious. On Sunday afternoon, when this became clear, my instinct had been to drop it quickly. In my experience religion is not good television material. It is too complicated and it takes up too much time. Trimmed into neat little ten-minute slots and labelled 'Epilogue' or 'Faith for Today' it becomes dull and insipid, a saucer of watery gruel offered to a hungry man. Introduced into a panel discussion or a report on current affairs it creates an atmosphere of frustration, damming rather than releasing the flow of ideas. It is both embarrassing and woolly and tends to involve the Corporation in tedious correspondence with viewers whose dogmatic fervour is equalled only by their total lack of charity. I would get no thanks from Patros if I turned in a highly-coloured essay on the theological problems of contemporary Judaism.

It was only gradually that we began to realize that what we were handling was religious in the ultimate sense of the word; a matter of life and death not peculiar to the Jews but affecting the self-awareness of every man. This was not an affair of priests or ritual—a squabble about ecclesiastical protocol, a heresy hunt down some obscure denominational corridor. This was concerned with the basic underlying question of human society—the meaning and nature of life itself. I suppose we should have seen it sooner. It was after all, stated simply and in the most vivid of terms. A man had been killed in the full vigour of life and was said now to have come back from the dead. Here, in plain black and white, was an enactment of the ancient human dream of immortality—the mythological break-out from the trap of history translated into reality.

If this were true it was, as Patros had said, dynamite.

Kapper agreed. "You'll have to play it down, Cass. Keep it smooth and casual. If you don't, it'll blow up in our faces." He shook his head. "As it is it's going to sound like episode six in a science-fiction serial."

I turned my head towards Number Two camera. "As of Friday evening the situation appeared to be well in hand. Following prompt action by His Grace the High Priest, working in co-operation with the Governor-General himself, the threatened revolution fizzled-out rather miserably. . . ."

The red warning light on the camera flicked off. I looked across to the monitor again, timing my words against the film clips Kapper had prepared.

"Scheduled to coincide with the annual Passover Festival it looked pretty menacing for a while. Just a week ago yesterday Jesus Davidson, the young rebel leader from Nazareth, made this triumphal ride into the city on a donkey. Puzzling as this may appear to many of us, it was a significant act in the eyes of the Jewish pilgrims crowding the roadside. Their tradition is that this will be one of the identifying marks of the Messiah—the God-King who will come to set his people free. . . ."

I had hoped for at least one good close-up of him here; something sharp and dramatic to fix him decisively in the viewers' minds. But all they could give me were medium shots across the heads of the crowd. You could see that he was tall and bearded, with broad shoulders and a high forehead. But that was about all. The black and white film robbed him of depth and personality. All that came through was a rather lonely figure seated awkwardly on a donkey, strangely unheroic in the storm of cheering.

"On Tuesday last he attacked the Jewish legal and ecclesiastical system at the heart of its organization—the great Temple of Jehovah. Here in the outer court there is something very close to open rebellion as he breaks through the mass of pilgrims and overturns the tables of the official money-changers, shattering their long-held monopoly. . . ."

Kapper had been quick off the mark with this clip. The camera looked down into the courtyard from a vantage point high on the walls and panned slowly over a scene of wild confusion. From that angle it was like watching the panic in a disturbed ant-heap. The sacrificial sheep and oxen had been turned loose among the people, their terrified bleats and bellows clashing with the screams of the women and the angry shouting of the men as they scrabbled for the spilled money in among the trampling feet and fought to protect themselves from being crushed against the walls. Overhead, blurring across the screen with the regular sweep of a radar scanner, a great cloud of pigeons wheeled and swooped.

"This looked like the preliminary move in a successful *coup d'état*. The conversion of the common coinage into the special Temple currency, with its accompanying heavy tax, has long been a source of resentment among the ordinary people who are forced to buy their sacrifices in the Temple market. After his action on Tuesday it was clear that in Jesus Davidson the working classes at least had found their long-awaited champion. . . ."

At the floor-manager's cue I came back on camera.

"Informed observers believe that if he had made his

bid at that moment nothing could have stopped him. If indeed his aim was to seize control of the government it is difficult to understand why he did not immediately exploit the situation. The authorities were helpless; the great mass of the people solidly behind him. The timing and the location were both perfect. The kingdom was his for the taking.

"But he didn't take it. He slipped away out of the crowd and disappeared. The moment of opportunity was lost. On Thursday evening he was arrested at a secret rendezvous outside the city limits, betrayed to the Sanhedrin, it is believed, by one of his closest friends.

"Sensitive to the electric atmosphere in the city, which at this time of the year struggles to contain ten times its normal population, the authorities lost no time in bringing him to trial. The Sanhedrin sat through the night and on Friday morning presented their verdict to the Governor-General. His Excellency signed the necessary order and Davidson was executed just before noon that same day. The revolution—if revolution it was—was over.

"Throughout Saturday's Festival Sabbath celebrations every precaution was taken to ensure that there would be no further incidents triggered off by supporters of the dead leader. At the end of the day the police were able to report that all was quiet. . . ."

Number Two camera came dollying in for a close-up. This was the critical moment—the introduction of the event which might well prove to be beyond the tolerance of the viewers; the switch from fact to what many would regard as being the wildest fantasy. I looked steadily into the lens and forced myself to relax.

"But early yesterday morning something happened at the tomb of Jesus Davidson. Just exactly what has been difficult to determine, but there was a disturbance of some

21

kind and the Jewish Army guard was badly rattled. The immediate result of this disturbance—whatever it was—has been a widespread and persistent rumour that the dead man is somehow alive again. . . ."

Spoken quietly, almost casually, in the tone of voice normally associated with the reading of the weather forecast, the words still sounded utterly incredible. I remembered all Kapper's warnings and had a sudden mental picture, appalling in its clarity, of Patros's face, and felt a trickle of sweat run down inside my shirt.

"Anyone who witnessed Friday's execution and the subsequent burial of Davidson's body will find this hard to believe. But there is no doubt that something very strange is going on, and that the authorities, both Jewish and Roman, are being compelled to take it seriously. Shortly after nine yesterday morning the High Priest drove to the Residency and was in consultation with His Excellency for over an hour. Whilst no official statement has come out of that meeting we were privileged, later in the morning, to obtain a filmed interview with the Governor-General. . . ."

3

Kapper put down the phone and nodded. "It's on, Cass. Pilate'll see you in fifteen minutes. At the Residency."

"Well, that's a break. I thought he was strictly a no-comment man."

"Oh, he is. He is indeed. I doubt if even you will be able to get anything out of him."

"Then why agree to be interviewed?"

Kapper smiled. "He likes to do the right thing."

"Even if he makes a botch of it?"

"He won't do that. Always turns in a very polished performance. While he's actually talking it sounds wonderful. Man to man, straight-from-the-shoulder stuff. And of course he looks the part. It's only afterwards when you come to think about it that you realize he's said nothing at all."

I took Greg with me and one of Kapper's technicians called Dober. We were received by a secretary; a bored, rather delicious young man who showed us into a small library on the ground floor and gave us what he called 'a run-down on H.E." while Greg and Dober were setting-up the lights. From the tone of his voice it was clear that he classified us as a necessary evil—like electricians or interior decorators.

"H.E. likes to keep things informal," he said. "Within limits, naturally."

I looked at him coldly. "I'm not planning to call him Ponty, if that's what's worrying you."

The secretary smiled wearily. "Quite so, Mr Tennel."

He watched Dober pulling the furniture about. "You'll put him behind the writing-table?" he said. "H.E. prefers to have something solid to lean on."

With the reputation he's got, I thought, that's understandable.

Jerusalem was a dead-end posting; the graveyard of many political careers. Nobody had been surprised when they gave it to Pontius Pilate. Everything about the man made him a natural for the job; his vanity, his arrogance, his incurable habit of vacillation, the long trail of expensive diplomatic blunders behind him, and of course his unfortunate marriage. After years of feeling his way across the quicksands of private censure and public contempt he would grasp at anything, even a writing-table, that could give him the illusion of security.

"We'll put him behind bars if you like, chum," Greg said.

Tall and thin, with a thatch of fair hair and freckles across the bridge of his nose, Greg Dekka at twenty-six still looked as though he had just left school. We suffered his rather pert sense of humour for the sake of his quite brilliant camera technique.

The secretary looked at him with distaste and inclined his head. "That will not be necessary, thank you." He glaced at his watch. "H.E. has a busy day scheduled," he said. "If you're ready now. . . ?"

Dober pressed the switch and the room blazed with

24

lights. Greg checked his meters, made a couple of adjustments, and nodded for the lights to go off. "Okay," he said. "Let's have him."

The secretary brought him in and made the introductions. Pilate shook hands and gave us what was obviously his number one Public Relations smile. As Kapper had said, he looked the part. In his middle fifties, bulky and upright in a dark lounge suit and a white shirt with the coveted blue and gold tie of the Praetorian Guard, he looked the epitome of authority, his silver-grey hair brushed back in wings, the straight Roman nose supporting a broad forehead. Seen in a long shot on some state occasion, or briefly in profile at a Summit Conference, he had sufficient physical presence to appear impressive. But face to face and in close-up his eyes betrayed him. They were brown and a little too small for his face, and sly. It was not the slyness of the shrewd negotiator accustomed to taking the jack-pot whatever his hand, but a slyness born of bewilderment and failure; as though a thirteen-year-old boy, trapped in the uncertainty of adolescence, lived inside that distinguished body and peered out at the world from his prison of fear. Here was a man who would ask questions not to discover the truth but simply to gain time to wriggle out of a dilemma; a man who would fumble in a crisis and then put his foot down hard on some trivial issue.

We settled him behind the table with the crowded bookshelves as a backdrop; did a brief voice-level test; switched on the lights and began.

"Lord Pilate," I said, "would you care to make a comment on this new crisis?"

He responded immediately to the title. Relaxed and smiling, he radiated confidence. "Certainly, Mr Tennel. But it's not a crisis, you know. Nothing like one. Every-

25

thing is under control. There's absolutely no cause for alarm. None whatsoever."

"That's good to know, sir. But there is this rumour about Jesus Davidson. . . ."

He came down quickly on that. "Davidson's dead. Dead and buried. I can see no point in discussing him now."

But I was not to be warned off quite so easily. "The rumour is, sir, that he's alive again."

His smile altered subtly, becoming one of amused tolerance. "Alive again? Oh, come now, Mr Tennel, really you know. . . ."

"Still alive then, put it that way."

He leaned forward, clasping his hands on the table, his face suddenly grave. "Mr Tennel, he was executed by soldiers of the Tenth Legion. They're not amateurs, you know. They're some of the toughest troops in the Roman Army. When they kill a man, he's dead and he stays dead."

"I quite agree. On the other hand, the rumour is very persistent."

"But of course,"—and back came the smile, dead on schedule—"this is Jerusalem, my dear chap. The Middle-East. We thrive on rumour here. It's meat and drink to these people. We're in the middle of a great religious festival. The Jews are an emotional people. Work it out for yourself, Mr Tennel. Of course there are rumours—and very splendid some of them are too. But when you've lived here as long as I have you'll not worry your head about bazaar gossip."

I nodded encouragingly. Not that he needed encouraging. If he had been half the statesman he was actor he would never have been thrown on the scrap-heap of Jerusalem.

"And what is your view of the incident at the tomb this morning, sir?"

Predictably he raised his eyebrows. "I'm afraid I don't quite follow you, Mr Tennel."

"The earthquake and so on."

"Oh, that." There was the smile again, tinted now with polite disinterest. "I believe there was a slight tremor just before dawn. It's the season for them, of course. Nothing remarkable about that."

"They say it was quite a big one."

"Do they indeed? I didn't feel it myself."

"Sleeping the sleep of the just, I'm sure, sir."

It was the first prick of the knife and he didn't like it. The bored smile vanished and his eyes were wary. I hoped Greg had him in close-up.

"Er—quite so," he said, and his voice was far from happy.

I decided to press a little harder. "Still, it was big enough to burst open the tomb I believe."

"Oh really? How very unpleasant."

It was beautifully done, with exactly the right inflection. If I pursued this line the viewers would think of me as a ghoul. I switched quickly. "Would you care to comment on the behaviour of the guard?"

He shrugged. "It was—unfortunate."

He looked at me hopefully but I refused to help him. I knew that if I kept quiet he would feel obliged to add to his answer. It is the first rule of interviewing. Almost anyone can give a brief answer. It takes a great deal of self-confidence to sit quietly and refrain from adding anything. More self-confidence than Pilate had. After a moment or two he said: "Not our chaps, of course. Jewish Army. Good lads, all of them. But a little—well, inexperienced."

I said, "You mean they panicked?"

"Panic's a strong word. Too strong, I think. Shall we say there was some—confusion?"

"Lord Pilate, why was it necessary to mount a guard over a dead man?"

He leaned back, giving himself time. "That's a good question."

"And the answer?"

"I'm afraid the answer is rather complicated. A matter of religion largely."

"Oh?"

He nodded. "Jewish religion. They take it very seriously you know."

"But how does religion come into it? I thought Jesus Davidson was a political prisoner, executed for high treason?"

"Indeed he was. He claimed to be the king of the Jews. That was his big mistake. It made him a direct threat to the security of the State. I gave him all the help I could. Bent over backwards to give him a chance to clear himself. But it was no use. He claimed to be a king and there was no getting round that. In the end I had no choice but to sign the execution order."

I understood now why he had agreed to be interviewed. Watching him leaning forward, gazing earnestly into the camera, I saw him as he saw himself—the conscientious, humane administrator struggling, in a difficult situation, to give every man a fair hearing and dispense justice with mercy. And then I looked at his eyes and the splendid image blurred.

I said, "And the religious angle, sir?"

"Ah yes. He was something of a fanatic about that I'm afraid. It made the whole affair rather—er—delicate."

His eyes, watching me unhappily, pleaded with me to leave it there.

I said, "In what way?"

"Well, he claimed to be not only a king but also—well —God."

"I see."

"Very embarrassing for everyone concerned. Especially His Grace the High Priest."

"Lord Caiaphas?"

He nodded. "A very distasteful business for him, as you will appreciate."

So that's how it was, I thought. The Church versus the State. Caiaphas holding a pistol to Pilate's head and young Davidson done to death to save the Roman's face.

"You say he claimed to be God?"

"Yes," Pilate said, and smiled. "Hence the guard."

"I'm sorry to be stupid, but why 'hence the guard'?"

"It's fairly obvious, surely? The High Priest insisted on it. You see, Mr Tennel, killing a man is one thing; killing God is something else again. If you kill God then you must take precautions. You've no guarantee that he will stay dead. So you must guard his tomb."

"And come down hard on rumours of a resurrection?"

"Exactly." He was smiling broadly now, man to man and no nonsense. Even his eyes were smiling, as though the extreme cynicism of his words had somehow given him fresh strength and confidence.

"Sir," I said quietly, controlling the disgust in my voice, "what did you think of Jesus Davidson?"

The smile disappeared abruptly. "I was sorry for him," he said. "Good material, but unbalanced."

"You think he was insane?"

He shook his head. "I wouldn't go so far as to say that.

29

But there was something strange about him—a sort of fatalism—a remoteness."

"A death-wish, perhaps?"

"Something like that. He made no attempt to defend himself, you see. I tried to get him to understand the seriousness of the position, but he seemed oddly unconcerned. Just stood there and looked at me and said nothing."

"I expect he was afraid."

"No, he wasn't afriad. It would have been easier if he had been. More normal, anyway. But he wasn't. Just tired and—and remote. As if he had already come to the end of his journey and the trial and execution were unimportant details—the mechanics of closing the door and lying down to sleep. When he looked at me I had the curious feeling that he was sorry."

"For what he had done?"

"No," he said miserably. "For me."

I saw the shine on his forehead and knew it was not only the heat of the lights that was making him sweat.

"It was quite absurd," he said, and his voice which until now had been deep was suddenly just a little shrill. "He didn't seem to realize that he was completely in my power. That I had only to speak and he was a dead man." He leaned forward, his face drawn and pale. "I had no choice, Mr Tennel. No choice at all. I did everything I could for him."

This was the real man at last, without the actor's mask; the bewildered boy inside the public image.

"It's not an easy thing to condemn a man to death," he said heavily.

Especially when he's young, I thought, and you know he's innocent.

I said, "But sometimes necessary."

He grasped the straw eagerly. "The good of the State must come first, Mr Tennel. Whatever the cost."

Provided someone else is paying, I thought. Someone without influence and with no friends in high places.

"I appreciate that, sir," I said. "I think we all do."

"I hope so," he said, pleading with the unseen audience. "I hope people will realize how dangerous the situation was. Without firm action we might well have been in serious trouble by now."

"It's good to know we have men like you, sir," I said, playing his game and hoping people would look beneath the surface of the words. "Men of integrity who are not afraid to do their duty, however unpleasant."

I thought for a moment I had laid it on a little too thickly. He looked at me quickly, his eyes suspicious. But his vanity overcame his doubts and he managed a very creditable smile. "Thank you, Mr Tennel."

"So now everything's back to normal."

"Oh yes," he said, relaxing, "I think we can safely say that."

"There is this rumour, sir, all the same."

"Rumours are not important, Mr Tennel. Only facts. And the fact is that Davidson is dead."

"You think we've heard the last of him?"

"I do." He did his best to sound confident, but I was satisfied that his words would convince nobody.

"Well, thank you, Lord Pilate. You've been most helpful."

He looked over my shoulder at the camera and assumed his vice-regal expression—bland authority based on an understanding of the common man. "It's been a pleasure, Mr Tennel."

We decided to go out and get some shots of the tomb.

On the way we stopped at a little bar in David Street and asked for whisky.

"Powerful disinfectant, this stuff," Greg said. "I'm beginning to feel clean again."

"Did you get him in close-up when I had him worried?"

Greg nodded. "God, what a phoney the man is. It was like filming a commercial for tooth-paste. A smile for every occasion."

We ordered another round.

"I'd like to have met Davidson," Dober said. "Any enemy of Pilate is a friend of mine."

"Me too," Greg said. "Pity it's too late."

I looked at the golden spirit in my glass. In some parts of the Empire they call it the water of life and believe that to drink it is to taste immortality.

"Yes," I said. "A pity."

4

The small, sly eyes looked at me unhappily out of the monitor. "It's been a pleasure, Mr Tennel," Pontius Pilate said.

I took my cue and turned to Number One camera. "That's the Governor-General's view of the situation. Everything is normal. There is no cause for alarm. Davidson is dead and the crisis over. These are reassuring words and everyone here would like to believe them. But the fact remains that Davidson's body has disappeared. The tomb, so carefully sealed and guarded, is empty. . . ."

The tomb was in a private garden outside the city; a pleasant place of trees and grass and the little flowers of Spring. It was a rather pretentious structure, a small mausoleum built of marble in the Greek style, with steps leading up to the portico and pillars supporting the roof. The massive stone slab designed to seal the entrance had been jerked back out of its groove. Two of the pillars were badly cracked and looked dangerous, and some of the roofing tiles were missing.

Greg whistled. "When they hang me, Cass, make sure it's in Jerusalem. We don't run to tombs like this for criminals back home. Just a hole in the prison yard and a couple of sacks of quicklime."

They had roped off the area and little groups of sightseers were bunched along the ropes staring at the tomb and keeping a cautious eye on the soldiers. Greg filmed a couple of brief sequences to set the scene for the viewers. One or two of the spectators moved hurriedly out of range, but most of them just stood and looked uncertainly at the camera.

We stepped over the rope and walked across the grass to where an officer was standing beside a jeep talking to the sergeant of the guard. He broke off as we approached and frowned at us.

"Yes?"

He was hard and weathered, with a big hooked nose and thick lips, his skin coarse and tanned by the desert sun. Fiercely correct in khaki-drill with two rows of ribbons on his shirt he obviously had little time for civilians.

"Morning, Major," I said. "We're from ITC."

"I don't much care where you're from," he said. "But you're out of bounds here. This is a restricted area and I must ask you to leave immediately."

He turned his back abruptly and said something to the sergeant, who saluted and marched off towards the tomb. I checked the list of names Kapper had given me. "I'm looking for a Major Sanballet," I said.

He turned quickly. "I'm Sanballet."

I nodded. "My name's Tennel. We've just been talking to the Governor-General about this morning's incident. You were the officer in charge of the guard detail I believe?"

"I was."

"I'd rather like to ask you one or two questions."

He glared at Greg who was busy with his cameras. "Is it official?"

I smiled. "More or less. We're doing a programme on. . . ."

"I have nothing to say."

"Does that mean that you have something to hide, Major?"

"No, it does not."

"Well then," I said, "there's no problem, is there?"

His heavy brows came down in a quick frown. I had to fight an impulse to stand at attention.

"Look here, Mr Whatever-your-name-is, I. . . ."

"Tennel. Cass Tennel. It won't take long. Five minutes. Ten at the outside."

"It's not on, Mr Tennel."

"No?"

He shook his head. "No."

I nodded. "It's your decision, of course. Presumably the Governor-General will understand your refusal to co-operate. I must confess I don't."

He looked at me, his eyes hot and angry. "So that's it, is it?"

"Yes, Major, I'm rather afraid it is."

He stood for a moment tapping his stick against his leg.

"I don't much like a gun at my head, Mr Tennel."

"I'm sorry," I said. "But I have my orders, just as you do."

"I could run you in right now for trespassing."

"But you won't." I smiled at him. "Major Sanballet, on the face of it, your troops have come out of this morning's incident rather badly. I'm giving you the opportunity to set the record straight. Do you really think it will help if I have to go on camera tomorrow evening, right after the Governor-General has finished speaking, and say that you refused to make any comment?"

He nodded. "All right. But keep it short."

Dober had the tape-recorder ready on the bonnet of the

jeep. I took the microphone from him and nodded to Greg. As the camera started turning I said, "Tell me, Major Sanballet, what exactly did happen here this morning?"

"There was an earthquake. O-four-hundred hours."

"A severe one, would you say?"

"I've seen worse."

"You were actually here, were you?"

"No. I was in the main guard-room."

"Back at the barracks?"

"Yes."

"I see," I said carefully.

He glared at me. "As guard commander that was my proper place of duty."

"Oh, quite. But who was in charge here at the tomb?"

"Sergeant Backra. Captain Yacoub was visiting."

"Making his rounds, in fact?"

"Yes. He was Orderly Officer."

"Does that mean he witnessed the earthquake personally?"

"It does."

"Ah. And would it be possible for me to talk to him about it?"

"Afraid not. Sorry."

"Any special reason?"

"He's—not available."

"Oh? Was he injured?"

"No."

"I see. What about Sergeant Backra and the rest of the guard detail?"

"Not available."

"So there was some trouble?"

He said stiffly, "There was no trouble."

"But there's going to be?"

36

"I don't understand you."

His speech was clipped and incisive, each word a curt explosion of sound. It was rather like interviewing a machine-gun.

I said, "Is it true that the men panicked?"

"Certainly not."

"No?"

"There was no panic."

"Then, Major," I said. "what did happen? Something went wrong. What was it?"

"I can't discuss it," he said fiercely.

"I see."

He scowled at me. "It's classified information. You'll have to wait for the findings of the official enquiry. I'm sorry."

I smiled. "Don't apologize, Major. I fully understand, and I'm sure the viewers will too. Tell me," I said quickly, before he could interrupt, "who reported the incident to you, Major?"

"Incident? What incident?"

"The earthquake. What else?"

"Captain Yacoub. On the walkie-talkie."

"Did he seem shaken at all?"

"He was concerned, naturally."

"About what?"

"The welfare of the men."

"And the fact that the tomb had burst open?"

"That too," he said stiffly.

"It certainly took a hammering."

"Yes."

"You came down straightaway, of course. What was happening then?"

"Nothing. Sergeant Backra had rallied the men. Everything was quiet."

"Ah," I said. "They needed to be rallied, did they? But when you arrived everything was normal?"

"Perfectly normal."

"But the tomb was empty?"

He hesitated, as though for a moment the gun had jammed.

Number one stoppage, I thought.

"Yes," he said then. "It was empty."

"You checked on that, of course?"

"Naturally."

I said, "Any chance of our taking a camera inside there now?"

"Afraid not. Place is unsafe. That roof could come down any minute."

"Um," I said. "It's a pretty elaborate sort of tomb for a criminal, isn't it?"

"Built for someone else."

"Oh? Who?"

"The Reverend Mr Joseph. He's the rabbi at Arimathea."

"Was he one of Davidson's supporters?"

"Hardly likely. He's a member of the Sanhedrin."

"Is he indeed? An influential man, then?"

"Yes."

"And he used his influence to give a traitor a decent burial?"

"Apparently."

"That's odd, isn't it?"

"Perhaps."

He eyed me warily. I signed to Greg and we got him in close-up.

"So when you got here the body was missing?"

"I've already told you that."

"And what's your explanation of it, Major?"

He frowned at the camera. "It's all in my report," he said, and clamped his mouth shut.

"I'm sure it is, Major," I said, and waited a moment or two without any real hope that he would add anything. This was a disciplined man, untroubled by silence.

"Major Sanballet," I said then, "what is your opinion of Jesus Davidson?"

But he was ready for that. "I'm a soldier, sir," he said. "I have no opinions."

"Oh quite. But you are also a Jew. And surely as a Jew you must have some theory about a man who dared to call himself God?"

"That's blasphemy," he said curtly.

"Yes," I said. "But why did he make such a claim?"

"He was mad."

"Just—mad?"

"That's what I said."

"Um," I said. "It sounds like an epitaph. 'He was mad'."

"If you like."

"I suppose it is an epitaph, Major? I mean, you're quite sure he is dead?"

He looked at me angrily. "Quite sure."

"Yes," I said. "Well, thank you, Major."

We humped the equipment over the rope to the car. Greg got out his cigarettes and we sat smoking thoughtfully.

"Talkative type, the Major," Greg said. "I wonder what he did put in that report of his?"

"Whatever it was," I said, "it's given them the shakes."

5

Sanballet came through magnificently, more Roman than the Romans, the epitome of military rectitude. Watching him on the monitor I could almost hear the drums and fifes. His final angry: "Quite sure" cracked out like a parade-ground command and gave me the perfect lead in.

"But the city," I said on cue, "is not so sure. During the morning the rumour strengthened as more and more pilgrims went out to see the empty tomb and came back wondering. Down the twisted streets and in the squares the tension began to build up. .

"Shortly before noon His Grace the Lord Caiaphas, High Priest of Jewry, convened an extraordinary meeting of the Sanhedrin.

"The Sanhedrin is composed of a group of priests holding what might be called Cabinet rank. Backed by the enormous weight of the ancient Mosaic Law it constitutes the most powerful ecclesiastical bloc in the Province, controlling the religious and social life of the nation with absolute authority.

"The meeting was held in the Quorum Room at the Palace. The Press and Television News were not admitted. However, we took our cameras down there and were fortunate enough to intercept one of the Sanhedrin members as he was leaving afterwards. . . ."

Dwarfed by the Temple, the High Priest's Palace was still an impressive building fronting on to a broad, paved terrace and flanked by walled gardens. A shallow flight of steps led up to the terrace and up again to the main doors which were massive and sheathed in copper. Above the doors a balcony stood out from the blank grey wall with a great Star of David embossed in gold leaf on its white marble facing. The doors themselves were kept by a section of the exclusive Temple Guard, hand-picked men superbly uniformed in the full-dress purple tunic and trews, with white wool-lined cloaks buckled about their shoulders and the distinctive cockaded hat adding to their height.

Driving through the city we were aware of the excitement building-up in the streets. The shops were open and there were plenty of people about, but nobody appeared to be buying anything. On almost every corner there were groups standing on the edge of the pavement; not shouting or demonstrating; just standing, like people waiting for a procession. In the street below the terrace of the Palace quite a large crowd had gathered to watch the arrival of the priests and to wait for their re-appearance. The police were very much in evidence, cool and efficient in their khaki-drill with the big service revolvers strapped to their belts. But there was little for them to do. The people were quiet; tense rather than rowdy; expectant and just a little afraid. Moving slowly past them in the car I was reminded of the feeling you get when there is to be a total eclipse of the sun.

We parked at the edge of the pavement just short of the terrace steps. Greg went to work immediately, filming the crowd and the Palace, while Dober checked over his tapes and the microphone lead. Kapper had provided us with special passes and we were allowed on to the terrace itself. Mordach of Syndicated International was there together with Jim Frood of Athens Universal and two or three of the local press-men. They were standing over on the right and they waved and nodded but made no attempt to come across and join us. They had all the writer's instinctive suspicion of TV and I knew that as soon as the meeting broke up they would go in like wolves to try to scoop us.

Just after two the great doors were swung open and the guards stiffened as the priests began to emerge. I had hoped they would be robed to fit the splendour of the setting, but they were in mufti—black suits and black homburgs. They came down the steps on to the terrace, packing together as the reporters swarmed round them flourishing notebooks and shouting questions. Greg was taking long-shots, waiting for me to butt my way into the huddle. But I stood still and let them get on with it. I was gambling on there being a straggler we could have to ourselves.

The priests moved away along the terrace, shaking their heads unhappily at the yelping press-men, making for the private gate into the Temple precincts. There was some desultory clapping from the crowd and one or two half-hearted attempts at booing. It looked for a moment as though we were going to miss out completely. And then our straggler slipped out quietly through the open doors and came down the steps directly towards us. I grabbed the microphone from Dober and moved to cut him off.

"Excuse me, sir."

He turned quickly and I found myself looking into a lined, scholarly face, the lips thin above the heavy beard, the eyes deep-set and shadowed with fatigue.

"Shalom, my son," he said. His voice was cultured, gentle and mellowed by prayer. "May you have peace."

"Shalom," I said.

He walked on two or three paces and I fell into step beside him. "I wonder if you would mind answering one or two questions?"

He stopped and looked past me at Dober and Greg. Down in the street the crowd was thinning rapidly, encouraged politely by the police.

"Questions?" he said. "What sort of questions?"

I smiled. "Perhaps we could begin by asking your name?"

"My name is Nicodemus," he said. "But I don't quite see how I can. . . ."

"The Reverend Jacob Nicodemus?"

"Yes. I am he."

This was a welcome bit of luck. Kapper had given me brief notes on most of the Sanhedrin members. With one or two exceptions they appeared to have been chosen for their extreme conservatism; men who could be relied upon in any emergency to toe the party line. Jacob Nicodemus was one of the exceptions.

"Not that he's a rebel," Kapper had said. "But he has what you might call a sensitive conscience. It has been known to get him into the odd spot of trouble."

I said, "Mr Nicodemus, let's go into the garden, shall we? It'll be quieter there."

I put my hand on his elbow and steered him off the terrace. Greg and Dober followed us discreetly. The path curved under the shade of some trees to where a small fountain was playing in a setting of grass and flowers. I stopped there and moved a little to my right, bringing him round to face the camera. Behind my back I signalled to Greg to begin filming.

For the benefit of the viewers I said, "Mr Nicodemus, you are a member of the Sanhedrin, are you not?"

"I am."

"I wonder sir—can you say a word about this morning's meeting?"

"It would be most improper for me to do so."

"Was any decision made, say at the political level, about the reported re-appearance of Jesus Davidson?"

He shook his head. "I am a simple priest, my son. I know nothing of politics."

He looked mildly at the microphone in my hand and up at the camera. His manner was so innocent, so gently courteous, that I was almost persuaded to call the whole thing off; cut the camera and thank him and let him go. I think if his coat has been even a little shabby or his cuffs the least bit frayed I would have done just that. Like so many of my contemporaries who have rejected the dogma of organized religion I tend to be absurdly sentimental about poor priests. Not princes of the church—I am unrepentantly atheistic in their company and enjoy nothing more than the destruction of their pride in front of the camera—but humble men in second-hand suits. There is something about them—a quality of transparent sincerity that slips under my guard and disarms me. They are at once so vulnerable and so strong; not sheltered from the world but involved in it and yet at the same time untouched by its stain. I cannot accept their beliefs which seem to me to be wholly irrelevant to the problems of the modern world. But they themselves impress me. They shine in the muddy sediment of life like grains of gold in a washing-pan, as hard to find and as easily lost. When I meet one I feel protective towards him. Not guilty, but protective. And just a little envious. It is like meeting a part of one's childhood again—the picture-book that has lain forgotten for years under the pile of old papers in a cupboard, the prize essay written at the

44

age of thirteen when everything was logical, seen with absolute clarity in terms of black and white. These things, like the humble priest, speak of another world from which we have been banished—or perhaps from which we have banished ourselves. It is no longer a world in which we could be content. But it is the only world in which we ever knew satisfaction, for it is a world in which belief and reason were one.

Looking at Jacob Nicodemus reminded me of that world. He stood by the fountain in that quiet garden, a simple country priest who had been elected to the Sanhedrin in recognition of devoted service in some obscure parish, and who now found himself involved in matters of policy which he did not understand. Everything about him added up to a humble, sanctified poverty. Everything —except a certain worldly wisdom in his eyes, a shrewd awareness in the set of his head, and the fact—in my view the damning fact—that he was dressed very expensively indeed.

I said, "The meeting was about Jesus Davidson, I take it?"

"He was discussed."

"But not as a political figure?"

"We are priests, not statesmen. Our concern is with faith rather than politics. Affairs of state we leave gratefully to Rome."

Fair enough, I thought, but you won't get Pilate to believe that. Not after what happened last Thursday night.

I said, "You discussed him as a religious figure, then?"

"You might say that. Yes."

"And will a statement be issued covering the religious implications of a resurrection?"

He raised his eyebrows. "I don't imagine so. The im-

45

plications of such an event are theologically obvious enough."

"In what way?"

"The power to conquer death belongs only to God."

"I see," I said. "That's quite definite is it? There are no doctrinal loop-holes that . . . ?"

"It is axiomatic."

I smiled. "Thank you, Mr Nicodemus. So if, in fact, Davidson is alive then the inference is that he is God?"

"It would be," he said, changing the tense neatly. "Yes."

I nodded. "And what would be the theological implications of that, Mr Nicodemus?"

He blinked at me mildly. "They would be tremendous, of course. Unprecedented."

"Is that what you've been discussing this morning?"

"Not really, no." He looked down at his feet.

I said slowly, "Is he alive, sir?"

He tried to smile, and failed. The tip of his tongue ran along his lips and there was a small flicker of fear in his eyes. Not doubt. Fear. The fear that leaps in a man who has built his life on a single idea, devoting his time and his mind to the understanding of it, and who suddenly suspects that he has been wrong. Not totally, gloriously wrong, but wrong in some apparently trivial detail which now seems frighteningly significant. I remembered some lines of Hebrew poetry I had once read in connection with a programme on the arts:

> *The stone which the builders rejected*
> *Has become the head of the corner.*

Watching the fear in the eyes of Nicodemus I found them peculiarly apt. This was no country priest over his head in matters he did not understand. This was a clever man—a scholar with a conscience—who understood only too well and was frightened by his knowledge.

"Alive? How can he be alive?" he said, and it was a question he put to himself rather than to me; a metaphysical question that had suddenly, incredibly become pragmatic.

I let him worry at it for a moment.

"I'm told you opposed his trial last Thursday night. Is that true?"

"Certainly not." There was genuine indignation behind the words and it supplanted, momentarily at least, the fear. "My endeavours were solely to ensure that the trial was properly and legally conducted."

"Of course. But it is common knowledge that your views were not shared by the majority of your fellow-members."

"In the Sanhedrin we are free to express our convictions openly. Only so can justice be done."

"It is said that His Grace the High Priest was in direct conflict with your opinions on that occasion."

"Is it indeed?" he said, with just the right amount of disinterest.

"Mr Nicodemus," I said. "Do you think justice was done—to Jesus Davidson?"

"To the best of our ability, certainly."

"He was properly convicted on sound evidence?"

"The evidence was heard."

I looked at him hard. "That is not what I asked you, Mr Nicodemus."

He frowned. "I have no wish to appear awkward," he said, "but would you mind very much not calling me 'Mr Nicodemus'? I'm accustomed to being addressed as 'Rabbi'."

"Of course, Rabbi. I'm sorry."

47

"Thank you.,'

Good try, your Reverence, I thought, but I don't snub that easily.

I said, "This matter of the evidence, Rabbi. Was it satisfactory?"

"There were many witnesses to testify against him."

"And did their testimony agree?"

"Substantially, yes."

He was taking it seriously, I could see that. Being honest in his answers. Standing there in the sunshine and working through it all again in his mind. Rehearsing the doubts he had experienced at the trial. Making every possible allowance for what had been said and done. I realized that it was important to him not merely to convince me of the justice of the trial, but also to convince himself.

"Substantially," I said. "But not completely?"

He looked at the camera and away again quickly. "There were some small discrepancies—minor details of no real significance."

"But big enough, perhaps, to hang an innocent man?"

He took it like a blow beneath the heart and reacted with anger. "That is a most infamous suggestion."

"I beg your pardon, Rabbi. You say there were many witnesses against him?"

"Yes. He had not been particularly discreet."

"But none to testify for him—is that not so?"

"That is correct. It. . . ."

"Bit unusual, isn't it, Rabbi?"

"There was no need of witnesses. He convicted himself."

"You mean he confessed?"

"It was more than a confession. It was a proclamation." He shook his head. "He said very little. But what he did say was completely damning. He made it impossible for us to save him."

"I see. So you agreed with the verdict?"

"It was the verdict of us all."

"No dissentients?"

"None."

I signalled to Greg for a close-up. "Did anyone abstain from voting?"

"You have no right to ask that question."

The fear was there, big now, only just under control. I pressed him quickly. "Did you, Rabbi? Did you refuse to vote for his death?"

He looked at the camera like a bird at a snake. "Yes," he said, his voice very low. "I refused to vote."

I nodded. "It was a blasphemy charge, wasn't it?"

"He claimed to be the Son of God. That was why we were powerless to save him."

I said gently, "Did you want to save him?"

"Yes."

I let it hang in the air for a moment, a small syllable of regret that faded slowly into the sound of the water splashing in the fountain.

"Does God have a son?" I said then.

"So we believe. We call him, 'He who shall come'."

"The Messiah?"

"That is his name."

"And what will be the purpose of his coming?"

"To bring life," he said simply.

"Life?" I said. "But we have life already."

He shook his head and smiled, a warm, natural smile. We were moving into familiar territory now and the ground was firm under his feet. "No," he said. "We have only the illusion of life. A handful of years between birth and death."

49

I was not too sure where this was leading us but Toplou liked culture and I decided the programme could carry a little more of it yet.

"They can be good years," I said.

"Yes, for some perhaps. The rich, the powerful; those who have youth still, and hope. Although even for those the years are quick to pass and come in the end to nothing. But the others—the blind, the crippled, the poor who watch their children fight for bread in the street, the widow who weeps in the loneliness of the night, the husband whose wife is a leper, the mother with the idiot child— they are not good years for these."

He sighed. "There is a dream that all men dream," he said. "A dream of freedom. It haunts us because we are prisoners. Jew and Roman, pauper and king alike, trapped in the prison of the body. At the moment of our birth we are condemned to death. It is the awareness of this that makes us men and also destroys our manhood. We have the illusion of life, but life itself is beyond our reach. We see it through the windows of our eyes as the prisoner sees the world from his cell. See it, and long to possess it. But when we reach out to seize it—it slips through our fingers."

The Jews thrive on tragedy. They are nourished by melancholy. I found his ideas morbidly depressing but they acted on Jacob Nicodemus like an injection of adrenalin. He seemed to grow visibly taller and stronger.

"In the days of the Exile," he said, "when my people were held prisoner in Babylon, there was a man called Isaiah who understood these things. He was a scholar of the Church—what we call a prophet—and he saw the Exile as a symbol of the prison of death. He spoke of the Son of God—of Him who shall come—and he used these words to describe him: 'Behold my servant whom I up-hold, my Chosen One in whom I delight. . . .' "

His head was up now and he was intoning the words, standing by the fountain with the majesty of the Temple behind him and all the sombre pride of his race in his voice.

" '. . . I have given him as a light to the nations, to open the eyes that are blind, to bring the prisoners out from the dungeon and those who sit in darkness from the prison-house.' "

I was not sure what this would sound like framed in a nineteen-inch tube—melodramatic probably and a shade unconvincing. But there in the Palace garden, backed by the personality of the man, it was extremely moving. Far too impressive, in fact, to suit my purpose. I gripped the microphone tightly and forced myself to think of Greg with his camera behind me.

"Thank you, Rabbi," I said, forcing a note of bored indifference into my voice. "That's really very interest-ing."

It was unforgivable of course. A deliberate—indeed brutal—breaking of the mood, as crass as a guffaw in a funeral service. He turned his head away quickly, as though I had slapped him, and shrank into his clothes.

"Of course," I said, using the same voice, "I'm not competent to talk about the theology of this, but it seems to me that Jesus Davidson would fit very neatly into your description of the Messiah. I mean, this opening of blind eyes and so on. I hear he rather specialized in that sort of thing."

He was back on guard now. "There have been others before him who have performed similar acts of healing. But they were none of them the One for whom we wait."

"And neither was he?"

"No. In many ways he was a remarkable person, and for a little while some of us dared to hope that perhaps in him the hope of our people would be fulfilled. But we were mistaken."

"You're sure of that?"

"Quite sure."

It was what Pilate had said, and Sanballet. On their lips too the words had sounded forced and unconvincing.

"Rabbi," I said, "what makes you so sure?"

His eyes met mine for a moment and then he looked down. "Because he is dead."

"Is dead? Or was dead?"

In the voice of a man reciting a formula he said, "The Messiah cannot die. The Messiah is the conqueror of death, the giver of life."

"I understand," I said. "There's just one small point I'd like your help with."

"Yes?"

"You've said the charge against him was one of blasphemy."

"That is correct."

"And yet he was executed as a traitor, an enemy of the State rather than of the Church. Can you perhaps explain how a man charged with blasphemy can be executed for high treason?"

He ducked his head and his voice was suddenly old and frail. The fear was about him like a cloak and all his pride was gone.

"It was . . . that is, I think . . . it was a . . . a . . ."

"A put-up job to get rid of him?" I said brutally. "Is that what you mean?"

"I . . . er . . . I don't. . . . Let me pass, please. I have a great deal of work I must . . . I'm sorry but you must allow me to leave . . . I cannot answer any. . . ."

I stood aside and smiled as he walked past me towards the camera and beyond it.

"Thank you, Rabbi," I said softly. "Thank you very much indeed."

6

We got back to the studios around three, dropped-off the film for processing, and went up in the lift to Kapper's office. He had laid on sandwiches and beer and we relaxed in the cool of the air-conditioning and listened to a play-back of the tapes we had made. It was an oddly depressing experience. Like an abstract painting the words demanded attention but gave nothing tangible in return. What did come through, and overpoweringly, was the stench of collusion and betrayal.

At the end Kapper sniffed and shook his head. "Poor devil. He hadn't a ghost of a chance against those boys." He sat back in his chair and clasped his hands behind his head. "Still, it makes life easier for us, Cass."

"In what way?"

"Well, it's obvious, surely? We just run a straight-forward political story. A sincere but naïve idealist attempts a *coup d'état*, only to have it nipped smartly in the bud by an administration that's had years of experience in dealing with this sort of thing."

"You mean we should take Pilate at his word and heave a big sigh of relief?"

"Why not?"

I got up and walked across to the window. Outside, the city was quiet; grey and enduring in the afternoon heat.

I said, "It's too tidy, Nick. And it begs too many questions."

"I've seen smoother jobs, certainly. But not from Pilate. Compared with his usual efforts this is a masterpiece."

Half-a-dozen kite-hawks were circling lazily above the Temple market. Over the Residency the Imperial flag drooped with indolent arrogance in the tired air. God was in his heaven, all was right with the world. And if putting things right sometimes meant that you had to use a little legal double-talk, select your evidence carefully and engineer the death of an innocent man—well, it was common knowledge, wasn't it, that this was far from being a perfect world?

I said, "A masterpiece of diplomatic murder."

Behind me Kapper said quietly, "All right, Cass. I agree. It's a dirty business."

I turned and faced him. "But it won't be, will it, by the time we go on camera tomorrow evening? We'll have worked it over by then, trimmed it and polished it and given it the good old ITC stamp of approval. It won't be murder then. It'll be an act of statesmanship. Stern, of course. Even regrettable. But just."

He raised his eyebrows. "What's the matter, Cass? Why so touchy all of a sudden? I don't like what they've done, nor the way they've done it. But it's done, for better or worse. As I see it, we've no option but to back them up."

In spite of the air-conditioning the room smelled stale. I had a headache and I was tired. All my experience told me that Kapper was right. What we had to do was to turn in a tidy little factual report that would satisfy Patros, give Pilate some much-needed support, and keep the Jewish authorities happy. Technically there was no problem. The film and the tapes could be edited to play down the nervous uncertainty in Pilate's voice and gloss over the unhappiness of Jacob Nicodemus. With a little skilful scripting I could make it all sound quite admirable.

But something at the back of my mind insisted that this was not good enough. I remembered the long-shot of Davidson in the film-clips Kapper had run through for me earlier. That lonely figure remote in the cheering crowd. And I saw again Pilate's sly, unhappy eyes pleading with me not to press him too hard in front of the camera. Perhaps they had been right about Davidson. Perhaps he had become too dangerous to be allowed to go on living. I didn't know, and I didn't much care. I knew only that they had trapped him somehow in a tangle of legal niceties, hustled him through a mockery of a trial and strung him up quickly—much too quickly—before anyone had had a chance to protest. I didn't care what he was— heretic, rebel, religious maniac. I was damned if I was going to let them get away with legalized murder without making them sweat a bit first.

I said, "I'm sorry, Nick, but it won't do."

"I see," he said, his voice ominously calm. "May I ask what you suggest as an alternative line?"

"I don't know yet. I want to do some work on this. Dig down a bit deeper into it. Find some of Davidson's friends, perhaps, and listen to their side of the story."

"And what good d'you think that will do?"

"Well, at least it might give us the real reason for his execution."

"I can tell you that now and save you the trouble. He was executed for treason."

"Ostensibly, yes," I said. "But you know as well as I do there's more to it than that."

"If there is, we can't touch it."

"Why not?"

"Because it's religious."

56

I shrugged. "So?"

Kapper sat forward quickly. "For God's sake, Cass, you don't need me to remind you of the official policy. Religion is out. The screen can't carry it except in very small doses properly labelled. Especially Jewish religion. This Messiah stuff's damned dangerous. It's broken Pilate and killed Davidson and a dozen others before him. If you let yourself get involved in it it'll finish you."

I said, with a casualness I didn't feel, "That's a chance I'll have to take."

He looked at me incredulously. "You can't be serious?"

"Why not?"

"You mean you're prepared to risk your professional reputation for the sake of some cock-and-bull story about the resurrection of a man you've never even met?"

I grinned. "It won't come to that. I simply want to see a bit of fair play here, that's all."

He shook his head irritably. "Look, didn't Patros tell you this thing's political dynamite? It only needs somebody to put a foot wrong and the whole country'll go up in flames." He leaned forward, his hands pressed flat on the desk. "As soon as I heard that rumour this morning I knew we had to move fast. That's why I got on the teleprinter to Rome. I knew how short the fuse was and how quickly it would burn. When I heard Patros was sending you I thought we had a chance. Cass Tennel, I thought, he'll known how to handle it. Get a proper story sorted out in no time and make short work of any nonsense about dead men coming back to life." He looked up at me sharply. "Because that's what we want from you, Cass. Patros and the Foreign Office boys and me. A nice, neat, no-panic piece that puts the whole thing into perspective and gives the political temperature a chance to subside." He sat back and turned his hands palm-upwards in a curious little gesture of appeal. "And that's what you've got, damn it. On those tapes we've just heard. Plain statements of fact from the State, the Church and the Army—all the right people. All you've got to do now is tidy it up a bit, feed in some local colour, and you're home and dry."

He frowned, his mouth puckering in disgust. "But now it seems that won't do for Tennel. Not Cass Tennel, the champion of lost causes, the poor man's hero with the over-size conscience. He wants to dig deeper. Stir up a lot of half-baked superstitious muck that nobody in his right mind'd take seriously for a moment. And then sit on camera tomorrow night, with all the world and his wife watching, and prattle about missing bodies and empty tombs and people gallivanting round the place when they've been dead three days."

"Now wait a minute, Nick," I said. "I'm not saying. . . ."

"No," he said. "You're not. Not on my programme."

He was really very angry indeed, clutching his temper with both hands and only just managing to hold it.

I said, making my voice mild, "It's my programme too, you know."

"I know," he said. "You're Mr Big. You go in front of the cameras and get all the kudos. But I'm the producer and I carry the can. When the bottom falls out of the stock-market and there's a run on the banks because you choose to treat rumours as though they were facts, it's not your head Patros'll be screaming for, it's mine."

I shrugged and turned back to the window. High over the city a couple of jet fighters spun their cotton-wool threads against the sky.

Behind me Greg cleared his throat warningly.

"You wouldn't always think so," Kapper said, "from

some of the stuff that gets on the screen, but we do have a certain responsibility to the viewers. I mean, it ought to be possible for them to distinguish between science-fiction and documentary."

"I said, "I hate to state the obvious, but the tomb is empty and the body is missing."

"Well?"

I turned and looked at him. "I think we've got to tell 'em that. Whatever line we take tomorrow night, I think that's got to go in."

Kapper sighed. "All right. No problem there. The body's been stolen—probably by his friends."

"Then why don't they say so? Pilate and Caiaphas—why don't they issue an official statement to that effect?"

"They will, Cass. They will. Give 'em a chance. They're probably working on it now. There was a guard on that tomb, remember. A Jewish Army guard. They've got to find some way of explaining how the body was stolen that doesn't make the Jewish Army a laughing-stock in every Roman mess from here to Britain."

He had a point there. It would explain the angry reticence of Major Sanballet, and also, to some extent, Pilate's uneasiness. But I thought of Nicodemus, shaken and evasive in the garden. He didn't seem to me to be the sort of man who would worry all that much about the army's reputation.

I said, "You may be right. It sounds logical enough. But I'm still not satisfied. There's something wrong somewhere. Something they're trying to hide because it frightens them. I want to know what it is before I commit myself to going along with Pilate."

Kapper's eyes sparkled with annoyance. "I've told you, leave it alone. If you go poking your nose into it you'll only make a bad job worse."

"I'm sorry, Nick."

"Oh well, of course," he said bleakly, "that makes everything fine, doesn't it?"

"If I might make a small suggestion. . . ?"

We had forgotten about Greg and turned now to look at him. Sprawled in his chair he smiled apologetically. "Instead of going round in circles biting each other's tails, couldn't we do something constructive?"

"Like what?"

He spread his hands, his eyes innocent. "Like finding Davidson's body, perhaps?"

Kapper stared at him for a moment and then said, "Of course. The boy's right, Cass. Find the body. It's the obvious move."

"Just an idea," Greg said. "They come to me occasionally."

I said, "That's nice. And how d'you suggest we set about finding it?"

"I can probably help there," Kapper said. "We've one or two useful contacts in the city and. . . ."

He broke off as the phone on his desk rang. "Kapper here. . . . Who? . . . Yes. . . . Yes, he is." He held out the receiver. "For you."

"Tennel," I said.

"You the chap that comes on the telly?" It was a man's voice, hoarse, urgent.

"Yes."

"Looking for Jesus Davidson, aren't you?"

"Well, I. . . ."

"Found him yet?"

"Look," I said. "Who are you?"

"Ah. No names, no pack-drill. Right?"

"All right. But. . . ."

"Had a go at Jacob Nicodemus, haven't you?"

60

"I've talked to him, yes."

"Get anywhere?"

"Not so's you'd notice."

"Ah," he said. "You wouldn't either, boyo. Not with him. Proper old belt-and-braces boy, Nicodemus is."

"Belt-and-braces?"

"That's it. Safety first. Take no chances. You know."

"I see."

"You want to talk to the right people, boyo."

"Such as?"

"The Magdala, maybe."

"Who?"

"The Magdala, boyo. She's the one that knows."

"And where do I find. . . ?" But he had hung up and the line was dead.

"Pro Bono Publico?" Kapper said.

"Constant Viewer himself." I jiggled the phone and got the switchboard. "That call that just came through. Can you trace it for me, please? . . . Thanks." I replaced the receiver. "She's going to try."

"Something worth following-up?"

"I don't know. It might be. Who's the Magdala?"

Kapper looked at me sharply. "The Magdala?"

"Know her?"

"I know of her. Why?"

"Our anonymous friend says she can tell us where to find Davidson."

"You mean the body?"

"Not the body. The man himself."

Kapper grinned. "The Magdala can?"

"That's what he said."

"Did he tell you what she is?"

"No. what?"

"She's a belly-dancer."

"Yes please," Greg said, and made kissing noises.

"At least," Kapper said, "she was. Worked in one of the cabarets down in the Old Quarter."

"And very nice work too," Greg said.

"The Army boys thought so certainly. And the tourists."

"I'll bet," Greg said.

"Other people were not so sure. This is a highly-religious community, remember. The Sanhedrin tends to frown on a young woman who makes her living by rotating her pelvis in public."

I said, "You say she was a belly-dancer. Does that mean she retired?"

Kapper nodded. "Disappeared. About a year ago I suppose it was. One week she was there, giving the boys a thrill. The next, she'd gone." He shrugged. "There were all sorts of rumours, of course. She was dead. She'd been offered a contract by one of the big-time clubs in Alex. Even that she'd entered a religious order."

"But no facts?"

"None."

"And since then?"

"Nothing."

"Um," I said. "Well, it sounds as though she's back in town. The character on the phone seemed pretty definite."

"If she is, she's not dancing," Kapper said. "We'd've heard."

"Maybe not," I said. "Belly-dancers are two a penny here, aren't they?"

"Not her class they aren't. She was something special. We'd've heard quick enough if she'd come back to it." He looked at me doubtfully. "I must say, Cass, she seems an unlikely source of information about Davidson. Especially if, as you seem to think, he's really a religious figure."

"I know. But we've tried some of the obvious people and got very little change. I think we ought to have a talk with Miss Magdala."

"I'll second that," Greg said, "with the greatest possible pleasure."

Kapper pursed his lips. "Worth a try, I suppose. Trouble's going to be finding her. He didn't give you an address?"

"No."

The phone rang again.

"May I?" I picked up the receiver. The girl on the switchboard was apologetic. They'd traced the call to Jericho to a public phone box. I was not really surprised.

"Jericho?" Kapper said. "That's interesting."

"Oh?"

"Look, Cass, Davidson went down well in Jericho. He was there less than a month ago and they really passed the hat round for him. Cheering crowds in the streets, official welcome by the mayor—the full VIP treatment."

"Any special reason?"

"No. Not really." He shrugged. "They're like that down thère, of course. Easily excited and unpredictable. Comes of living below sea-level I suppose, and breathing air that's three parts pure sulphur. Anyway, he had the town in his pocket until. . . ."

"Yes?"

Kapper shook his head. "He was an extraordinary man. Time after time he'd get the people behind him. Walk in from nowhere and start talking. God knows where he got his ideas from but they were good. Damned good. And he could put them over too. Ten minutes on his feet in front of a crowd and they were eating out of his hand. He could pull 'em in, and he could hold 'em. But he couldn't go on from there. Just when you'd think nothing could stop him, he'd fade out. Pack up and walk away and leave 'em hanging in mid-air. Either that or else he'd do something stupid. Some little ill-considered thing that would set them all against him. Like in Jericho. He walked in just before lunch and by mid-afternoon it was his town. He could've asked for anything and they'd've given it to him. Any mortal thing. Instead of which he picked the most unpopular man in the place and invited himself to dinner with him. Turned his back on the crowd and snubbed the city fathers and went off arm-in-arm with Zaccheus."

"Zaccheus?"

Kapper nodded. "The local Quisling. Runs the tax office in Jericho. Everybody hates him. He's been robbing 'em for years. Lives like a king and chucks money about like water. And it's their money, and they know it's their money, but they can't do a thing about it."

"And Davidson stayed at his house?"

"Yes. God knows why. If he'd searched for a year he couldn't have found a worse man to be friendly with." He spread his hands. "It wasn't the first time he'd played his cards badly. Seemed to have no clue about people. Hopeless judge of character. Curious failing in a man so talented. Fatal one, too." He rubbed his finger thoughtfully along the side of his nose. "This laddie who rang up just now—did he have a throaty sort of voice? Gravelly, with a rasp in it?"

"Yes, he did."

"I wonder if. . . . Did he call you 'Boyo'?"

"Yes."

Kapper nodded. "It's a long shot, but it might have been him." He looked at his watch. "Why don't you and Greg take a run out to Jericho and have a crack at him? I'll get the address for you. He might be more forthcoming face to face. Meanwhile I'll do some checking at this end. See if we can track down that Magdala girl for you."

I must have looked a bit doubtful because he smiled and got up briskly. "Don't look so worried, Cass. We'll get there yet."

I nodded. It wasn't the getting there that was worrying me. It was what we would find when we got there.

7

On the monitor screen the garden of the High Priest's Palace had all the delicate beauty of a Japanese print—the trees making a frame within the frame, the fountain playing in the sunlight—with the oddly impressive figure of Jacob Nicodemus standing at the focal point. Impressive even in the incoherence of the final moments of the interview, when he appeared to rush upon the camera like a black, angry bird, his face blurring as he came too close to focus, the dark bulk of his body blotting out the scene.

"Thank you, Rabbi. Thank you very much indeed."

I listened to my own voice tying the last sardonic knot and took my cue on Number One camera.

" 'The Messiah cannot die. The Messiah is the conqueror of death.' These are the words of one of the Sanhedrin's leading rabbis—a learned man well-schooled in the theological mysteries of his people. For him, at least, the death of Davidson last Friday afternoon would seem to rule out any possibility of him being the Messiah. But what about the people themselves? Do they also accept the fact of his death as final?"

Kapper fed in some film of the crowds in the streets and even in the miniature black and white pictures the sense of expectancy came through with surprising strength.

66

"Three days after his death the streets are full of people. Why? What are they waiting for? And whom do they expect to see?"

They cued me back on camera and I half-turned my head towards the huge panorama of the city behind me.

"To discover the answers to these questions we went to find some of his friends. Some of the ordinary citizens of Jerusalem living in this tangle of narrow alleys—men and women who knew him well enough to share a meal with him and, on occasions, give him a bed in their homes.

"It proved to be a difficult search. The men who were closest to him—men like Peter Johnson and the Zebedee brothers—are in hiding. The authorities are taking no chances and have put a price on their heads. They have not been seen since Friday afternoon. The strong line taken by His Excellency Lord Pilate, and the refusal of the Jewish leaders to comment, have made people reluctant to talk, especially to strangers. We were a long time finding a lead.

"When we did it was not in Jerusalem at all. It was in Jericho."

Driving down to Jericho for the first time in the late afternoon was not an experience I will easily forget. The first three miles were unremarkable. The road climbed steadily round the shoulder of the hill, running up through the dusty olive groves to Bethany. In spite of its romantic name (the House of Song) Bethany was nothing special to look at. Just another fly-blown collection of labourers' cottages strung untidily along the roadside, the whitewash flaking off their mud-brick walls, the usual clutter of rubbish decaying on their flat roofs. But the setting was superb.

The road turned sharply at the end of the village, beginning its long, twisting drop through the barren hills to the valley of the Dead Sea far below. It was like driving over the edge of the world. Behind us were houses and grass and trees, the familiar dress of an inhabited land. In front of us, abruptly, desolation.

The vastness of the view gave it an appalling majesty. We looked over the bonnet of the car down a huge ruined staircase of boulder and scree that fell steeply, mile after naked mile, to plunge finally into the steaming pit of the world's lowest valley. No grass grew there, nor any tree. There was not à house nor a flower nor a sign of human habitation. Only the broken rock-slides and the naked road and the dead wood of the telegraph poles climbing up to meet us, joined together by their thin wires like the skeletons of ancient mountaineers.

This was the watershed of Jewish history. Down this escarpment Abraham had sent his young men to rescue Lot from the terror that fell upon Sodom and Gomorrah, those ill-sited cities of the plain whose ruins lay crumbled now, choked in the chemical mist that drifted over the barren water of the lake. Up over this savage terrain the army of Joshua had swarmed, gaunt and hard from the desert years, caked in the bloody dust of shattered Jericho, and driven by a religious spur which rowelled their minds as they struggled to earn the approval of their newly-discovered God. The sunlight that flashed innocently now on the windows of our car as we swung round the hairpin bends had burst in a thousand splinters on their spears and arrowheads, and the little pennant of dust flying in our wake was like the ghost of that rolling dust-cloud through which they had marched with the Ark of the Covenant bruising their shoulders. To the people of the olive groves above and behind us, watching them emerge from the head of the gorge, they must have seemed like devils from the centre of the earth.

The mountains of Moab, marvellously close and golden in the shimmering light, rose above us against the sky. Somewhere in that jagged desert wall, in some forgotten ravine known only to the eagles, their first great leader slept in an unmarked grave. Moses, who had brought them out of Egypt and given them not only the Law but also a dream of God which had created a nation out of a rabble of frightened slaves. A dream which had bred David and Elijah and Isaiah the prophet; which Babylon had been unable to break and Rome could only just hold in check. A dream of holy freedom which haunted men like Jacob Nicodemus and had entered into the son of a village joiner and destroyed him.

But had it destroyed him? Or had it found in him, at last, the one who could contain it?

We sat silent in the swaying car watching the shadows rising darkly like water in the valleys below us. The towering walls of the mountains seemed to lean inwards, compressing the tired air. I looked at the needles of the instruments quivering like nerves on the dashboard and tried to think of the questions I would put to Zaccheus of Jericho. But the deadness of the world outside the car infected my mind. My thoughts drifted like smoke, elusive, insubstantial, without form or meaning. I remembered the story of Orpheus and his desperate journey into the underworld. It was down such a corridor as this that he had travelled to find his wife and bring her back to life. But in spite of his courage and the beauty of his music there had been no resurrection for her. . . .

I looked at the film clips of Jericho that Greg had taken, waiting for my cue from the floor-manager. The camera

69

ranged down the length of the Street of the Sun, the broad main avenue that ran through the heart of the modern city from the ruins of the ancient fortress that had fallen to Joshua, to the Jordan bridge. The street was tree-lined and shaded, with one or two impressive public buildings. In the civic square there were flower-beds and an unusually fine fountain. On the screen it all looked spacious and restful, but I remembered the heat rising out of the ground even in the shade, and the smell of sulphur in the air, and the sharp taste of salt that soured the water and ruined the flavour of the food. The salt and the sulphurous smell drifting over the streets from the pewter-dull lake, and the flies. The flies were bad in Jerusalem. They were infinitely worse in Jericho. Big and heavy and disgustingly slow, they crawled over the food, clustered thirstily round the eyes of the children, and rose in buzzing indolent clouds when they were disturbed.

The floor-manager dropped his hand to cue me.

"From here, only three weeks ago, Jesus Davidson set out on what proved to be his last journey to Jerusalem. The journey, as we know, ended in tragedy. But it began in triumph. The people of Jericho lined the streets under these trees to watch him go by, cheering and clapping the man whom they believed to be a prophet and a liberator, the long-awaited champion of the common man."

There had been plenty of people about when we drove into the city. The afternoon siesta was over and the shops were busy. Watching the monitor now it was easy to visualize that earlier occasion—the crowd cheering to see the latter-day Orpheus, whose words had charmed them into new hope, starting his long journey back up that terrible valley to the heights of the capital.

"Among them was a man called Zaccheus. Mr Regem Zaccheus, head of the Jericho taxation department."

His face appeared in close-up on the screen with an almost physical impact. It was an astonishingly ugly face, the skin pocked and scarred, stretched tightly over lumpy cheek-bones and falling in loose folds of fat about his jowls. Above the wide mouth, fringed with grey whiskers, his huge nose jutted aggressively, a white pad of scar tissue ridged over an old break across the bridge. Heavy black brows formed a continuous line across his forehead. His hair was coarse, springing angrily out of his scalp and sprouting in tufts from his ears and nostrils. The whole face was a mask of power and cunning; a ruthless face belonging to a man without pity. Until you looked at his eyes. They were large and lustrous, velvet dark, as eager as the eyes of a child. There was something child-like too about his manner; a quality of innocent excitement that was immediately communicated even through the monitor. It was as though, within the grossness of his body, he lived in a world of music and laughter; a fresh, singing world wherein all men were free.

We had filmed the interview in his house in Jasher Street. A big furniture van was parked outside when we arrived. We stood waiting while three men in sacking aprons manhandled a piano down the front steps and into the van. The house was a blaze of lights and we followed a trail of straw up the path and in through the front door. There were packing-cases standing open in the hall and two more removal men pushed past us with a sideboard. Somebody was shouting instructions at the top of the stairs and there was a noise of hammering from one of the bedrooms.

Zaccheus came out of a room on our right.

"Mr Zaccheus?" I said.

"In person, boyo. Come for the bedding, have you?"

"We're from. . . ."

"In there. All ready and waiting."

The man upstairs shouted down. "What about this carpet on the landing then?"

"Get it up. And the under-felt. It's to go in the van with the other stuff." Zaccheus grinned at us, rubbing his hands. "Everything must go. Owner leaving town. I've been on the blower to Matron over at the Children's Hospital. She's expecting you tonight with the blankets and things."

His voice was the same, hoarse and gravelly, the way it had sounded on the phone in Kapper's office.

"Mr Zaccheus," I said. "I think we ought to introduce. . . ."

"What's the trouble, boyo? Stuck for a bit of transport are you?"

"It's not that, But. . . ." I broke off helplessly as a man bobbed out of the room across the hall.

"What about these statues in 'ere, Guv?"

"In the van," Zaccheus said. "They're to go to the Gallery. And go easy with 'em, boyo. Couple of genuine Praxiteles there." He winked at us. "Little bit of extra dividend I picked up three or four years ago. Don't like 'em much myself, not to live with that is. But they're money in the bank, boyo. Money in the bank."

"Is there somewhere we can talk for a few minutes?" I said.

"Talk? What about?"

"Jesus Davidson."

He looked at me hard for a moment and then smiled. "Got you placed now. Thought I'd seen you before. You're that Tennel chap on the telly."

I nodded. "You rang me up this afternoon."

"And you traced the call, eh?"

"More or less."

72

"Good for you, boyo. I like a man with a bit of initiative. Find the Magdala, did you?"

"Not yet," I said. "I'm hoping you can help me there."

"Maybe. I dunno. Have to think about it." A man came downstairs with a roll of carpet and we pressed against the wall to let him by. "Nice bit of stuff," Zaccheus said. "Persian, of course. Nothing to touch it."

"You're moving house?" I said.

"You don't need brains to work that one out, boyo. We're going north, first thing in the morning. Galilee."

"And all this?"

"Giving it away. Every last stick and stitch of it. Furniture, books, carpets—the lot. Spreading it round the town a bit. Hospitals, Old People's Homes, Schools—that sort of thing."

We stood back in the doorway to let a large walnut writing-table go by.

"For the Mayor," Zaccheus said, "with my compliments. I've given him one or two nasty headaches in the past. That'll help to make up for some of 'em." He grinned and shook his head. "Taken me years to get this little lot together. Top-grade stuff, y'know, all of it. No rubbish. No sale-room junk. Every piece a collector's item. And now it's all going, in one night. Crazy, isn't it?"

"About our little talk. . . ."

He scratched his head. "Yes. Well. . . . Mind coming into the kitchen? Bit quieter there I daresay."

And that was where we filmed the interview. In the kitchen, sitting on a couple of hard chairs with the door shut and the muffled thuds of furniture being humped down the stairs as background noises.

I watched him now on the monitor as he answered my opening questions.

73

"Mr Zaccheus, is it true that you actually met Jesus Davidson?"

"That's right."

"You're one of his men, are you?"

He smiled, the ugliness of his mouth redeemed by the bright composure of his eyes. "In a way, yes, I suppose you could say that."

"Does that mean you believe in him?"

"It does."

"As the Son of God?"

"Certainly."

No hesitation here. No cautious qualifying clauses. He looked squarely into the lens and answered with a sort of reckless directness, relaxed, confident, completely natural. It was as though, having drilled through the hard rock strata of Pilate and Nicodemus, I had suddenly struck oil.

"Why?" I said. "Why do you believe in him?"

"He set me free," he said simply.

"From what?"

"From myself," he said, as though it was the most natural thing in the world for a crooked tax-man with a caricature of a face to discuss metaphysics in front of a television camera.

"How did he do that?"

"He forgave me. Met me in the street and accepted me, and forgave me for being the sort of man I am." He smiled. "I was up a tree. I wanted to see him go by. I was curious, see? Heard a lot about him. Wanted to see what he looked like. But they wouldn't let me through. I'm not what you'd call popular in this town. Can't expect to be, of course. I've milked 'em dry for years. Made no secret of it either. Been proud of it, as a matter of fact. Started from nothing and made my way up to the top. Made a lot of money doing

74

it, but no friends. So as soon as they saw it was me they bunched together and blocked my view. That's when I shinned up the tree. Just in time too. He was right there underneath me. There was a fair bit of noise—cheering for him, the other thing for me—and he looked up to see what it was all about. And he said, 'Well then, Regem Zaccheus, aren't you going to ask me round to dinner?' And you know something, boyo, it was the first civil word anyone'd spoken to me in forty-odd years."

I nodded encouragingly. Not that he needed to be encouraged. He was as eager to talk as Sanballet had been reluctant.

"I've come up the hard way," he said. "Left on my own at the age of five. No bedtime stories. No school. Nobody to put in a word for me. Talk about do-it-yourself." He shook his head. "I've worked for Rome most of my life, but I'm still a Jew, Mr Tennel. A son of Abraham. And we Jews have a law—'Love God and your neighbour'. That's what the law says. We don't, of course. We pretend to, but we don't. Can't afford to. It's as simple as that. A man has only so much love in him. Enough for himself and maybe a wife and the kids. Perhaps even a bit to spare for a couple of close friends. But no more than that. It isn't that he doesn't want to love his neighbour. It's just that he daren't let himself, because he hasn't enough to go round. Love's a luxury, boyo. I found that out very early in the piece."

In his ugly face his eyes were quiet and compelling. My mind reached out to Patros in Rome, willing him to listen. I knew with what impatience he would receive this kind of talk. Patros likes action. If, occasionally, he agrees to allow a little philosophy into a programme he wants it from a professional, not from somebody like Regem Zaccheus.

"The priests tell us the law comes from God," he said. "But if that's true, God's a luxury too. We can't afford him either. That's why we keep him in the church, the way some men keep art treasures in a museum. We can't afford him in our own homes. All we can do is go and look at him in church sometimes.

"Jesus Davidson now, he understood that. He was poor all his life. Started as a joiner, and there's no money in that. Never owned a house. Only had one suit. No car, no credit, no insurance. Nothing. Thirty-three years old and not a penny to his name." He raised his eyebrows. "Couldn't even afford to go and look at God in the Temple. Couldn't raise the price of the sacrifice the priests sell in the market as a sort of ticket to get in." He grinned at me happily. "Heard about that, I expect? About him tucking in to the money-changers?"

"Yes," I said.

He nodded. "Wish I'd seen it. Quite a party they reckon it was." He leaned forward, his face suddenly serious. "A man like that," he said. "You could trust him. He was really one of us, see? The sort of God the priests go on about was no use to him. Locked up in church, admission by ticket only. 'It's not my Father's house any more'—that's what he said." He jabbed his finger at the camera. "D'y'know what happened last Friday—when they hanged him? The big curtain in front of the Holy of Holies in the Temple split right down the middle. Ripped from top to bottom it was, and when people looked behind it there was nothing there." He grinned. "Shakes you, doesn't it, boyo? All these years we've been buying sacrifices to get in and stare at that curtain, gaping at it because the priests said God lived in there behind it. And all the time it was a swindle. Nothing there. Nothing but empty space and dust and a few cobwebs.

"He knew that too, of course. 'My Father's kingdom,' he said, 'it's all round you. In your town. In your house. In your hearts. You don't need money to get in—in fact people with a lot of money find it very hard to get in. All you need is love.'"

He was silent for a moment or two. Over our heads we could hear furniture being moved about and the tramp of feet on the stairs.

"It was the only thing he had," he said then. "Love. And that's what he gave me."

I could imagine only too vividly the impact of this statement on Television House in Rome. We have more than our share of queers there, especially in the News Department, oddly enough. Greeks mainly; intellectuals in revolt from the aggressive masculinity of Rome. Men of exceptional talent who called each other 'Darling'. The effect on them of this ugly little man talking so unself-consciously of the love of a Galilean joiner would be spectacular.

"He shared it with me," he said then, "Sat at my table and ate my food and gave me love. If you really want to know a man, that's the way to do it. Sit down and eat with him. That's what he did, boyo. It wasn't God in church any more, expensive and out of reach. When he came it was God in my house, making himself one of us, trusting himself of us like a friend."

Greg had him in close-up, the lights brilliant in his dark eyes as he smiled. "That's what love is," he said. "Trusting yourself to your neighbour. Laying yourself wide open for him to come in and help himself to what's yours. Not just money. Everything. Ideas. The things you hope for. The things you lie awake sweating about. You open the door and let him come in and look round. Talk about shewing your hand. You let him in like that, boyo, and you're really in his grip. Like that song, y'know, what's it called—Unconditional Surrender."

"A bit drastic, isn't it?" I said.

"Shakes you rotten, boyo, I don't mind telling you. Really goes against the grain. Like giving some character a loaded pistol and opening your coat and inviting him to have a go." He grinned, shaking his head. "Funny thing is, it sets you free. It doesn't matter any more, see? You've stepped out from behind the wall—out in the open. For the first time in your life you've had the guts to look at yourself as you really are. And it's like breaking out of jail, boyo. You don't have to pretend any more. You don't have to hide behind the front you've spent years putting up. You're free."

There it was again. The ancient dream of freedom. Pilate and Nicodemus had recognized it in Jesus Davidson and had been puzzled and afraid. Regem Zaccheus, seeing the same thing, had accepted it completely. For him, at least, it was magnificently real.

"Mr Zaccheus," I said. "What are you going to do with your freedom?"

"I'm going to live," he said, as though the answer were obvious; as though, in saying those four words, he had explained the whole purpose of man. I realized that he was using a new language; a religious language which employed ordinary words like love and freedom in an entirely new way. In his vocabulary these common words, worn thin and dulled in a million conversations, devalued in law-courts and business-houses, in shops, in television programmes and on political platforms, had become technical terms as esoteric as those used by the physicist and the mathematician. They glittered in his speech like freshly-minted coins, and it was clear that to him they were immensely valuable, full of a new, exciting meaning.

But what exactly that meaning was it was not easy to define.

I said, "I understand you're giving up your house here in Jericho?"

"That's correct."

"Literally giving it away?"

"Yes."

"And the furniture too?"

"House, furniture, bank account—the lot."

"Isn't that a little rash, Mr Zaccheus?"

"I don't think so, no."

"But surely your house and. . . ?"

"I don't need it, boyo. I don't need any of it. It was me, see? What I'd built up to give myself a bit of status. My personal answer to the men who'd done their damnedest to keep me down in the gutter. But now—well, it doesn't matter now. I don't need a house and money to make me somebody. I'm a person in my own right. I've got my freedom see? Complete and free. That's all any man needs. That's everything, boyo."

The way he said it, it sounded magnificent. And dangerous. I began to understand the panic in the minds of Pilate and the Sanhedrin. If Jesus Davidson could inject this sort of stuff into a man like Zaccheus and make it take he had clearly been a person to watch very carefully indeed. A person to watch, and, when the opportunity came, silence.

I said, "And where do you go from here?"

"Up north," he said, "to meet him again."

"Davidson?"

"That's right."

"And what will you do when you've had your meeting?"

"No idea," he said cheerfully. "That's up to him."

"Mr Zaccheus," I said carefully, "it sounds as though you're quite sure he's alive again."

79

"Oh, he's alive all right. No doubt about that. No doubt at all."

All of which was interesting but not especially convincing. Zaccheus believed in the resurrection. Nobody watching him could doubt that. But he hadn't witnessed it any more than I had. Davidson had been kind to him in the face of public opinion. Understandably he was prepared to go overboard for him now. But we needed something more factual than the loyalty of a friend, however shining that loyalty might be, if we were to persuade the viewers that Davidson was alive again. And when, before the interview, I had pressed him for facts, he had been very cagey indeed.

"This business about Davidson being alive again," I said. "Do you believe it?"

"Of course," he said.

The casual confidence of his answer irritated me. I was tired, and the kitchen was stuffy. I was in no mood to be patronized by a man like Zaccheus.

"There's no 'of course' about it," I said sharply.

"Why not? He said he would come back from the dead, and he has done."

"You were there when it happened, were you?"

"No."

"But you've seen him since?"

"Not yet."

I nodded. "So it's just a rumour."

There was a particularly heavy thud on the ceiling above our heads. He grinned and cocked his head. "That's my furniture going out, Mr Tennel," he said. "You reckon I'd let it all go on the strength of a rumour?"

"All right," I said. "So you've got some inside information."

"You could call it that."

"Reliable?"

"Safe as a bank, boyo."

"Who gave it to you?"

"The Magdala."

"You mean the girl who used to be a belly-dancer?"

He nodded. "She rang me this morning."

"And said he was alive?"

"Yes."

I said, "And that's what you call reliable information? A phone call from a cabaret girl?" I shook my head. "I'm sorry, Mr. Zaccheus, but you'll have to do better than that."

He shrugged. "Take it or leave it, boyo."

"Oh, come on," I said. "I can't go on camera tomorrow night and tell people Jesus Davidson is alive again just because you've had a phone call from a belly-dancer."

"I don't see what her being a dancer's got to do with it," he said. "She's seen him and talked to him. I reckon that ought to count for something."

"Seen him?" I said. "You mean, this morning?"

He nodded. "Five o'clock or thereabouts. In the garden, right outside the tomb."

"And you say he talked to her?"

"That's right. Gave her a message for all his friends. He wants us to meet him in Galilee."

"Mr Zaccheus," I said, "I've got to see this girl'"

He looked at me doubtfully. "I don't see why. I've told you what she said on the. . . ."

"Hearsay," I said. "It's not enough. I need an eye-witness to go in front of the camera."

"Well," he said. "I dunno, Mr Tennel."

I said, "She's in Jerusalem, of course."

"Yes. They're all there. The Magdala and Peter Johnson and the Zebedee boys—all of them. That's it you see. They're lying low at the moment, and that's all right. The tricky bit's going to be when they try to get up north, with the Sanhedrin and the police and the army all breaking their necks to get hold of 'em. I wouldn't want to say anything at this stage to make things tougher for them." He looked at me, his eyes suddenly hopeful. "You couldn't hold off for a bit? I mean, after this meeting up north we'll know better where we stand. Next week, say. That might be. . . ."

"Too late," I said. "The programme's tomorrow night."

He shook his head. "I don't like it, Mr Tennel. They trust me, see? I wouldn't want to betray their. . . ."

It took me another ten minutes to get him round. Even then he was ultra-cautious. Made me promise that if he gave me the Magdala's address I wouldn't put any pressure on her to go in front of the camera. Made me promise further that if she did agree to an interview I wouldn't reveal the whereabouts of the house where she was staying. But once I had given him my word he relaxed completely. He scribbled the address on a slip of paper and handed it to me.

"Thank you for trusting me," I said.

He smiled. "Don't thank me, Mr Tennel. Thank Jesus Davidson. His idea, not mine."

"I'd like you to tell me some more about him," I said.

And after that it had been plain sailing.

The last of the furniture was going into the van when we left. Zaccheus came out to the car with us and stood on the pavement while we settled ourselves in. I rolled the window down and put out my hand.

"Goodbye then, and thanks for all your help."

"You've got the address safe?"

I nodded.

"Don't forget, boyo. It's up to her whether she talks or not."

"That's a promise."

He gripped my hand hard. The light from the street-lamp etched his face in cruel relief, emphasizing the pitted skin, the great jutting hook of the nose.

"Shalom," he said.

"Shalom, boyo," I said. "May you live to climb many more trees."

He laughed then, throwing back his head and opening his mouth wide. Dober let in the clutch and we were away, leaving him standing there with the empty house behind him and the sound of his laughter echoing down the street.

"Quite a boy," Greg said.

"Yes."

"Never have taken him for a religious man myself."

"No," I said, and thought that we might perhaps have to revise our image of what a religious man was like.

8

"Oh, he's alive all right." Confident, almost cocky, the voice of Regem Zaccheus grated out of the monitor. "No doubt about that. No doubt at all."

It was a moment of great conviction, as decisive as a line drawn under a signature. A good place to make a break.

I sat back as the image faded and a white, five-pointed star exploded onto the screen heralding the commercials. The red warning lights of the 'Sound On' and 'Vision On' signs flicked out. One of the girls came forward between the cameras with a cup of coffee for me. I got up and stretched and moved out of the lights. The floor-manager joined me and we stood together sipping the hot drink.

"So far so good," he said.

As if on cue the phone on the desk rang. I walked over and picked up the receiver, bracing myself for the wrath of Patros. But it was only Nick Kapper speaking from the production box.

"Nice going, Cass," he said, which was praise indeed considering his sceptical view of the whole story. "Got somebody here who ought to clinch things for you."

On the monitor screen a man and a girl were locked in a close-up kiss against a background of violin music at the conclusion of an advert for somebody's mouth-wash. I waved my hand to have the sound turned down.

"Yes?" I said. "Who?"

"Chap called Cleopas," Kapper said. "Reckons Davidson was at his house last night. Had quite a session with him apparently."

"Genuine?"

"I think so. He's a perky little character. Transparently honest."

"Will he go on camera, d'you think?"

Kapper chuckled. "He'll go on camera. Problem's going to be getting him off again. He's been bashing our ears in here for the last quarter of an hour."

"Where is he now?"

"In the canteen. Miriam's taken him down for a cuppa. Want to use him?"

"I dunno, Nick. Have to do it off the cuff. Might be a bit tricky."

"Up to you, Cass. He's another eye-witness. I don't think you can afford to pass him up."

"I know," I said. "It's a question of fitting him in at this stage."

"Have to cut something, of course. What about that truck-driver laddie—what's his name again. . . ?"

"Didymus."

"Yes. I think you could lose him without weakening your case. Be a bit stronger with him out of it, actually."

I looked at the monitor and thought about this. They were showing a cartoon advertising refrigerators; the old classic with the little gremlins swarming all over last year's model, lighting fires in the freezer and sloshing buckets of water over the food racks with the dial set to de-frost. There was something compelling about their frenzied activity, but I wasn't really focused on the gremlins. I was seeing again the truck sagging under its towering load of timber and the stocky figure of Thomas Didymus in old jeans and a leather jacket arguing doggedly with the guards. . . .

It was half-past eleven on Sunday night when we swung left out of the Bethany road by Gethsemane and drove up the steep slope to the Damascus Gate. All the way from Jericho the road had been deserted, but as we topped the rise we could see the white glare of the arc lamps and the barrier-pole in position. It was like driving into a film-set. Against the backdrop of the gates set massively into the stone walls there were soldiers with sten guns and automatic rifles, and a little group of travellers bunched together under the lights by the truck. As we approached, a corporal stepped out of the hut by the barrier and stood waiting, his rifle ready. Dober slowed the car and stopped in the pool of light.

"Papers please," the corporal said.

I handed out our passports and priority passes. He checked them unhurriedly and gave them back.

"Thank you, sir."

"What's it all about?" I said.

"Routine security precautions, sir."

"Against what?"

He smiled, his young face bleak under the peaked cap. "Trouble. What else?" The hard light glittered on his brass cap-badge and shone with a cold sheen on the barrel of his rifle. "Returning to the studios, are you, sir?"

"Not yet," I said. "We have someone to see in the city first."

"Sorry, sir. City's out of bounds till morning. Nobody in, nobody out. Orders from the Governor-General."

"Yes, but look here," I said. "That is important. We're

doing a programme on the story of Jesus Davidson and we must. . . ."

"Ah," he said. "Then you'll know all about it, won't you, sir?"

"All about what?"

"The curfew, sir. Like I said, it's a routine precaution. People get a bit worked up sometimes. Do silly things. Need to be looked after. Protected from themselves, like."

Out of the corner of my eye I saw two more men take up their positions on the other side of the car. They were big men and they moved with a casual, almost indolent precision which I found oddly menacing.

Greg said quietly, "Tenth Legion, Cass. You'll get no change out of these boys."

I knew he was right but I thought it was worth another try.

"Look, Corporal," I said, "you've seen our passes."

"All in order, sir. We were told to expect you sometime tonight."

"They're special passes, you know. Priority."

"That's correct, sir."

"Well, then?"

He shook his head. "Sorry, sir. You can't go into the city tonight."

I looked past him at the huddle of people by the truck and the bold black stripes painted on the white wall of the hut. "Have you got a phone in there?"

He nodded.

"Mind if I use it? I'd like a word with your Commanding Officer."

He winced slightly. "Wouldn't do that if I were you, sir."

"Nevertheless I'd like to try."

"Can't stop you, of course, sir. But if you'll take my advice you'll. . . ."

"Thank you," I said, and got out of the car.

There was a list of numbers pinned to the wall of the hut above the phone. I got through to the barracks and asked for the CO.

"Who's calling?" The voice of the telephonist was wary.

I gave my name.

"I see, sir. Well, I'll put you through to the Orderly Officer."

"No," I said. "I want the . . ."

The phone crackled sharply and I heard the steady buzz of the ringing tone.

"Orderly Officer here."

"My name is Tennel," I said. "I'm with a special ITC team and . . ."

"IT who?"

"Imperial Television. I would like to speak to the Commanding Officer."

"Colonel Macer? You want to speak to the Colonel?"

"I do."

"Now?" Incredulity lifted his voice out its suave, no panic groove.

"Yes," I said impatiently. "Now."

There was a little pause. "What's it about, Mr Tennel?"

"It's a matter of some urgency."

"My dear chap, I should hope so. Nobody in his right mind disturbs the Old Man at this time of night for anything less than armed insurrection."

"Just put me through," I said. "I'll take full responsibility."

"I daresay, old boy. But it doesn't work out quite like that, you know. I'll have to ask you to be a bit more specific."

88

"Look," I said. "We're at the road-block by the Damascus Gate and we want to get into the city. It's as simple as that."

"Simple answer too, old boy. You can't."

"That's no good to me. I've got to get in tonight. There's somebody I have to interview for a programme. Urgently."

"Oh? Who?" His voice was suddenly crisp, interested.

"No," I said, remembering my word to Zaccheus. "I can't tell you that. Let me talk to the Colonel."

"I'll let you into a secret," he said. "The Old Man doesn't like TV. He'd eat you alive."

"I'll take that chance," I said.

Sorry. No can do, I'm afraid.

"You mean you won't put me through?"

"That's right," he said pleasantly. "Wait till morning, old boy. The gates open at five-thirty."

"Might be too late then," I said. "I told you, this is urgent."

"Sorry, old boy."

I played my last card. "When I spoke to the Governor-General this morning—he appears in the programme by the way—he was much more co-operative than you've been. Odd, isn't it?"

But he didn't even hesitate. "Yes," he said imperturbably. "Isn't it?"

I put the phone down and turned. The corporal was standing by the door of the hut. He raised his eyebrows. "No joy, sir?"

"No."

"Ah," he said. "It's a rough old world sometimes."

Greg was waiting for me by the barrier. "We're still on the outside looking in, I take it?"

I nodded. "Never even got to first base."

"Oh well, it was worth a try."

"Remind me to send a big donation to the Society for the Suppression of Orderly Officers, will you?"

"Be a pleasure," he said.

Behind him the great iron-studded face of the Damascus Gate loomed mockingly in the glare of the arc lamps. I looked at it bitterly. Somewhere in the maze of narrow streets behind it was our only eye-witness. But I had no real hope that she would still be there in the morning by the time we had found our way to the house after the lifting of the curfew. Half-way to Nazareth more likely, and impossible to catch up with in time for the programme.

"Pilate and his panic measures," I said. "They'll be jammed in behind there a good hour before the gates open. Packed in solid. We won't have a hope in hell of getting through to find her."

"Lose herself in the middle of 'em and slip through without being noticed if she's got any sense," Greg said.

He gave me a cigarette and held a match to it. "Going to be a long hard day tomorrow again, Cass."

I nodded.

"Meanwhile," Greg said, "we have a small consolation prize for you." He pointed towards the car. "See the chap talking to Dober?"

I looked at the short, solid figure; the faded jeans; the broad, dirt-streaked face under the lank hair.

"Doesn't look much, does he?" Greg said. "But he happens to be a bit special."

"Who is he, anyway?"

"Name's Didymus, of all things. Thomas Didymus. That's his truck with the timber trying to fall off it. He's a joiner."

"Fascinating," I said. "What am I supposed to do? Cheer?"

"Why not?" Greg said. "He's one of Davidson's boys."

The polysyllabics jumped across the monitor screen, blinding the credulous with pseudo-science in an advertisement for a detergent with a wonder ingredient guaranteed to wash clothes even cleaner.

"What d'you think then, Cass?" Kapper said.

I closed my eyes. The interview with Thomas Didymus had been strangely frustrating. We had been cleared by the corporal to take the ring road round two sides of the city to the studios, and had persuaded Didymus to go with us. In front of the camera he had talked readily enough. It was what he had said that had been disconcerting.

"I've nothing to hide, mister," he said. "He's dead and that's all there is to it."

This bald statement, delivered in a flat voice, shook me. The man was after all a close friend of Davidson, one of the Eleven who had been with him from the beginning. I had expected that he, at least, would vehemently support the resurrection story. But when I said as much he shook his head.

"It's been rough this last couple of weeks," he said. "Dead rough. Big strain on all of us. Specially the women. They've had about all they can take and then some. When people get hammered like that you're bound to have rumours floating round."

"You think it's just that? A rumour?"

"Wishful thinking," he said. "I saw him die, mate."

"It's not just the women, you know. Regem Zaccheus in Jericho is convinced that. . . ."

"Well, I'm not," he said doggedly. "Mary Magdala reckons she saw him this morning. Put her arms round

91

him, so she says. Talked to him and everything. Fair enough. When that happens to me I'll believe too. But until I see him alive and touch him—make sure it's really him—I'm not falling for any stories about dead men rising."

"But surely you were expecting him to rise? I understand that on more than one occasion he said he would come back from the dead."

"I daresay," he said fiercely, sitting tense in the studio chair, his big hands gripping the arms. "I'm not like you, mate, educated and that. Most of what he said was way over my head."

"But he did say that?" I said pressing him for an answer. "He did say he would come back?"

"Okay, yes. He said that."

"But you don't believe it's happened?"

"Not on Mary Magdala's say-so."

"His tomb's empty—you know that, of course?"

"Yes."

"Was it robbed, d'you think?"

He scowled. "Wouldn't be the first, would it?"

"But who would want to rob it?"

"I dunno, mate." His voice was flat, disinterested. Obviously, so far as he was concerned, the shutter had dropped on Friday afternoon. Anything that happened after that was unimportant and without meaning—the irksome details of probate and the disposal of possessions.

"It wasn't Johnson, was it?" I said. "Or one of the others?"

"Don't be bloody silly, mate," he said wearily.

I looked at him with sympathy. There was something compelling about his stubborn matter-of-factness; a quality of tough realism which marked him as being the sort of man who would be very welcome in a tight corner. And loyal. Desperately, doggedly loyal.

"You want him back, don't you?" I said. "You want him back and alive again?"

He nodded, his eyes sombre. "If you'd known him like we did. Lived with him for three years. . . ." He looked up suddenly, his face defenceless.

"We believed in him, see? We thought he really was God."

"Why? What made you think that?"

"If somebody turns up out of the blue and starts doing miracles, wouldn't you think he was God, mate?"

"Well," I said carefully, remembering Patros and the viewers, "miracles are not really my subject. I'd want to examine the evidence rather. . . ."

"You've never seen a miracle happen, have you, mate? Not heard about it from somebody who knows somebody who was there, but seen it with your own two eyes. You've never done that, have you?"

"No. No, I haven't."

He nodded. "Well I have, mate. Scores of times."

"That makes a difference, of course," I said, not quite managing to keep a trace of patronage out of my voice.

He picked it up at once and jerked his head in disgust. "Aw, come on," he said, "break it down, will you?"

"I'm sorry. I didn't mean to. . . ."

"We'd walk into a village, see? And there'd be a blind beggar by the synagogue, propped up against the wall, covered in flies and whining for a hand-out with a tin mug in his fist. And he'd walk across to the poor devil and just touch his eyelids and say a couple of words. And the chap'd open his eyes wide, like a little kid getting a present. And he'd be able to see, mate. No bother at all." He shook his head as if the memory still bewildered him. "Deaf men, cripples, lepers, chaps who couldn't speak—didn't make a ha'p'orth of difference what was wrong with 'em. Just a touch and a word and they were okay. Happening all the time, y'know. Not just now and then. Every day, mate. Every day that came."

"Yes," I said. "That's impressive, certainly."

"Impressive?" His eyebrows went up. "It was bloody wonderful, mate. Out of this world. I remember one time we were in a boat. Up in Galilee on the lake, see? Night-time it was and the wind dead against us. And he came walking on the water—just strolling over the waves the way you and me'd walk across a field. And another time we got caught out there in a storm. Blowing like the clappers and a big sea running. And he just spoke three words and it was all over. Wind dropped, moon shining, lake flat calm.

"When you've seen a man do things like that, mate, what else can you do but believe he's God?"

"But now," I said, "you've changed your mind about him?"

He looked at me bleakly. "He's dead, mate."

"And that makes a difference?"

"God can't die."

It was the same obstacle that had defeated Nicodemus. The cold fact of death beyond which no man could go.

"What was he like?" I said. "As a person, I mean."

"I dunno. Different. Not like other men."

"You mean he was a genius?"

"You could say that. Yes."

"Was he a good man, Mr Didymus? Clever, sympathetic, understanding?"

He frowned, looking straight into the camera but not focusing on the lens. "There aren't any words," he said slowly. "Good, clever—they don't begin to say what he

94

was like. Okay, he was all of those things— all the right things—but the words don't mean anything when you use them about him."

I said, "Well, what did he look like? I mean, was he tall, for instance?"

"He always seemed to be tall. When you were with him he sort of towered over you. And that's what I mean about words being no good to describe him. Because compared with a chap like Peter Johnson say, he was only average height."

I smiled. "They tell me Johnson's quite a giant."

"Yes," he said. "He's big. Over six feet and broad as a house. But when he was with the Master—I dunno— he seemed to shrink somehow."

"Is that what you called Davidson—the Master?"

He nodded. "You're a Roman and I'm only a Jew. A Yid. That's what you call us isn't it? Dirty little Yids."

"No," I said. "Please. . . "

"That's okay mate. You don't have to apologise. Names don't matter a damn anyway. You've taken over our country, but you haven't taken us over. We don't think of ourselves as Roman subjects, y'know. We're a free people, mate, and we don't call any man Master. But we called him that. Sounded right, somehow. Felt right too."

He looked at me defiantly. But behind the defiance there was a certain wistfulness, a naked longing for what might have been.

"Mr Didymus," I said, "what was it all about? What did you expect him to do?"

"Take over the Government, of course," he said. "What else? We thought he was Messiah."

"Is that what Messiah will do? Rule the country?"

"Not just the country, mate. The world. 'The government shall be upon his shoulder'—that's what we say about Messiah."

He was crouching in his chair, small and lonely under the lights. So ordinary, so insignificant a man, talking in a flat voice about world domination.

I said, "But surely you must've seen it was impossible? A village joiner and a handful of men against the Sanhedrin and Rome."

"Like I said, we thought he was God," he said doggedly.

"Yes," I said. "Of course." I waited a moment or two and then I said, "What happens now, Mr Didymus? Now that he's dead and you're on your own, is there any future for you? As a group, I mean."

He shrugged. "Doesn't matter now. It's all over. Finished."

"What will you do?"

"Go back to work. Pick up the pieces and start again."

But he could inject no enthusiasm into the words. For him, at least, the world had come to an end last Friday afternoon.

"What about Judas Iscariot?" I said.

He glared at me. "What about him?"

"He's dead too, isn't he?"

"Yes."

"Is it true that he sold Davidson out? Informed on him to the Sanhedrin?"

"The thing was finished," he said. "We all knew that. It was only a question of time. He made his bid at the Feast, and it failed."

"You mean when he rode into the city?"

"Yes. Then. I could've told him it wouldn't work. But he was set on doing it." He looked at me, his eyes dark and hopeless. "When he said he was going to try it we

96

knew it was the end of the line. They tried to talk him out of it, Peter and some of the others. We were holed-up in a cave above the Jericho road, and they spent hours arguing with him. But I could see it wasn't going to work. He was past listening to any arguments. The death-wish was on him and there was no escape—for him or for us." He shook his head. "Y'know what I said, mate? I said, 'Come on lads. He's going to get the chop and we've no choice but to go with him.'

"It's like you get with a tree sometimes. A big, tall tree that's been attacked by a bug. It's got to come down, mate. It may look all right, but inside the bug's eating the guts out of it. Nothing else to do but bring it down. Doesn't matter a damn who puts the axe in. The tree's had it, and that's all there is to it."

"But is that a fair analogy?" I said. "Surely he. . ."

"Look, mate," he said fiercely. "He said he was the Son of God, and we believed him. Well, he was wrong, that's all."

"You mean he was mad?"

It was the same question I had put to Pilate. What other question could you ask about a man who thought he was God?

"I dunno," Didymus said. "He might've been mad. Iscariot was dead sure he was."

"And that's why he went to the Sanhedrin?"

"Maybe. Part of the reason anyway. Iscariot believed in the Kingdom as much as any of us. More than some, perhaps. It might have been he thought the Master had gone over the edge and was in the way. I dunno." He shook his head in that gesture of weary bewilderment. "We weren't ready for him, that was the trouble, mate. We could hear him talking to us, and it sounded bloody marvellous. But what it meant was something we couldn't

97

sort out. Not even the brainy boys like John Zebedee and Iscariot. I reckon it broke him up in the end, trying to get through to us about life and freedom and the Kingdom, and us not being able to follow him. I reckon that's what killed him—not being able to make sense even to his friends."

I said, a shade sharply, "Oh, come now. There's no mystery about what killed him. He fell foul of the authorities, religious and political. The Sanhedrin framed charges against him and Pilate. . . ."

"That lot," he said angrily. "They don't count, mate. No more than Iscariot did. They didn't bring him down, don't you fret. He could've given them the slip any time he liked." He leaned forward and the lights threw deep shadows under his eyes. His face was like a tragedy mask outside a theatre. "No, it wan't Caiaphas and his yes-men. And it wasn't Iscariot sneaking off in the dark to grass on him. It was us, mate. Us, his friends. We killed him. He'd come to the end of the line, and he knew it. Played his last card and seen it go down.

"We all knew it was finished," he said. "Last Thursday night when we had supper with him. We knew then it was all over. The death-wish was on him so strong we could feel it in the room like a draught of cold air. I don't mind telling you, mate, we were scared out of our wits just being there with him. We sat and looked at each other—didn't dare look at him—and the food was dry and sour in our mouths. It was like eating with a dead man."

He was stumbling over the words now, groping his way through them like a man struggling to climb out of the ruins of a house that had collapsed on top of him.

"You know what he said to us, that night? He picked up the loaf and broke a piece off and handed it to us. And he said, 'Eat this. It's my body—myself—the real me—

98

broken for you.' And later, when the meal was nearly finished, he offered us wine. And he said, 'Drink this, all of you. It is my blood.' "

He ducked his head suddenly and covered his face with his hands. I heard the soft click of the camera as Greg revolved the lenses and went back to medium shot. Under the hot brilliance of the lights there was a sense of horror in the studio; a creeping shadow reaching out to touch us all. Resurrection or no resurrection, the presence of Jesus Davidson was there with us, conjured up by the lonely, sobbing man who had put down his saw and his plane to go out and follow a dream.

I could feel the whole beginning to sag in my hands. It was as though we were all—floor-manager, cameraman, sound technician—involved in a nightmare; a slow, grey unwinding of the spiral of hope. Beyond the bright circle of light the darkness was intense and menacing. I looked round quickly, feeling trapped and afraid, and saw the sweep second hand on the studio clock swinging remorselessly round the dial. I concentrated on the clock and felt the spell lift. I said, just to say something, just to get back to normal, "He must've been a remarkable man."

Didymus looked up then and I was shocked by the naked pain in his expression. "He died the next day," he said, his voice impersonal and without passion, curiously dissociated from the agony in his face. "He died on Friday afternoon. And we murdered him."

"He's a hostile witness, Cass," Kapper said over the phone. "Like I've said all along, I don't think you can afford him."

"I don't know," I said, feeling again that sense of pity and terror created in my mind by the words of Thomas Didymus. Was he really hostile? He had no faith in the fact of the resurrection of Davidson certainly. On the other hand, the man had had a tremendous effect on him. And something of the mystique of his personality came through in the story he had told me. It seemed to me that one fact stood out a mile, if Davidson had been the sort of person Didymus described, the only ending that would make sense of the story was a resurrection. I said as much now to Kapper.

"You may be right, Cass," he said. "But since when has history had to make sense? Whichever way you look at Davidson's story, it's a tragedy. And tragedy is, basically, the senselessness of life. A good man, full of high ideals, done to death by treachery and jealousy—that's tragic, and it simply doesn't make sense. Therefore it's convincing. People can recognize it as a mirror of their own experience. If you want to tack on a miracle at the end you can't afford to have Didymus saying his piece. It's too real and too likely. You'll never persuade them to accept your fairy-story ending after that."

"He knew Davidson," I said stubbornly. "And he was able to communicate something of the man to us. That's important, Nick."

"This chap Cleopas knows him too," Kapper said. "Knows him, Cass. Present tense. Not just knew him."

The floor-manager was making urgent signs to me to get off the phone. The commercial break was coming to an end.

"He's on your side," Kapper said.

"So's Didymus, in an upside-down sort of way."

"I don't see that, Cass."

"Well, look," I said. "The fact that he doesn't believe Davidson's alive is important. If they're trying to fake a resurrection—if they've pinched the body and are spreading a rumour about him, it's not very likely that one of them—one of the inner ring like Didymus—is going to sabotage it all with a flat statement of disbelief, now is it?"

"You mean, because Didymus doesn't believe it, it's more likely to be true?"

"Exactly."

"Um," Kapper said doubtfully. "Bit subtle for the viewers, Cass. I still think you'd be better off without him."

The floor-manager was drawing his hand across his throat and glaring at me.

"Well, come on, Cass," Kapper said. "Cleopas or Didymus, which?"

The cameramen were climbing back on to the dollies. The microphone dipped down over my head on the end of its boom. There was, as usual, no time to think.

"Both," I said firmly. "I need the two of 'em."

"No can do, Cass. You know as well as I do we're pushed for. . . ."

"I want 'em both, Nick. Get on the wire to Patros. Tell him we've got to have extra time."

"He'll never wear it."

"He's got to. This is a big story. I'm not going to have it spoiled for the sake of five minutes' extra time."

"Five minutes? He'll do his nut, Cass. You know what he's like."

"Tell him two minutes then. Once we get started he won't fade us out." I nodded reassuringly at the floor-manager. "Oh, and Nick, I want to do a switch now."

Kapper groaned.

"We'll have the Magdala film next. Then Caiaphas. Then Didymus. And I'll take this new chap at the end. Okay?"

"But Cass, you can't move Caiaphas. We agreed he has to have the last. . . ."

"Thanks, Nick. Sorry to be a bother."

I put down the receiver and took my place behind the desk. The last commercial flicked off the screen. The warning signs glowed. The floor-manager shook his head reprovingly and dropped his hand. I looked into the camera lens.

"We went next to see the Magdala—the girl who had phoned through to Regem Zaccheus in Jericho and told him that Jesus Davidson was alive again and wanted to meet his followers in Galilee. . . ."

9

As it turned out, my fears of not catching her before she left for the north proved to be groundless.

We dossed-down on camp-beds in Kapper's office and left a message with the switchboard to call us at five in the morning. But there was a slip-up somewhere and it was after six when the phone rang; and gone half-past by the time we got to the house in the Watergate. The city had been open for more than an hour and when we knocked on the door I had little hope of finding anyone in. But she was there.

Thanks to Pilate's curfew and the stubborn Orderly Officer we had missed the men. Johnson and the Zebedee brothers and the rest of them had gone at first light. But she was still there. She had decided to stay on for a couple of days, acting as a kind of information centre for anyone sympathetic to the cause. There were two or three other women with her in the house and she left them in charge and went back with us to the studios.

She was a little hesitant about coming with us at first, but when I explained that we had talked to Zaccheus she smiled and began to relax. I said we had also interviewed Thomas Didymus, and that seemed to clinch it. She asked what he had said, and when I told her, she nodded.

"We must put that right, at all costs, Mr Tennel," she

said crisply. "For Thomas's sake as well as for everyone else's. Whatever he finally decides to do we can't let him have that on his conscience."

I sat back now and watched the gaudy neon signs of the cabarets in the Old Quarter winking and blazing on the monitor-screen against a background of honky-tonk piano music. Some months previously the Jewish Mobile Film Unit had done a documentary on the night-life of the capital, and the library had provided us with this clip. Filmed around midnight, it showed the district at its hectic, vulgar worst, the camera lurching drunkenly through the crowds jamming the narrow streets, panning from side to side to give glimpses of the posters on the walls, the sweating faces of the men looking at the girlie photographs, the girls themselves in their tight skirts smiling in the doorways; probing through the blur of legs almost at ground level to pick out a clutch of broken bottles, a trampled forage cap, a woman's glove crumpled in a puddle of vomit. The Miramar, the Silk Stocking, the Tambor, the Pantie Club—the names of the cabarets were a litany of lust chanted mutely by the flashing lights as the camera dipped and swayed down the length of one street and up the next in a sort of ritual dance and came to rest staring up at a huge plywood figure of a nearly nude girl straddling the doorway of one of the biggest of the clubs.

Kapper had insisted on having this particular sequence in. Watching it now I was still dubious about it.

"Contrast," Kapper had said. "The programme needs it, Cass. In among the priests and the penitents, a little honest dirt. Nothing like it to keep the customers happy."

The customers, and probably Patros, who would smack his lips greedily over this sort of stuff. Whether or not the programme needed it was another matter.

The camera butted its way in through the tiny foyer, past the grinning faces of half-a-dozen soldiers, to the cabaret itself. The zoom lens carried us over the heads of the audience, pushing aside the shadows and the drifting cigarette-smoke and focusing on the small, brilliantly-lighted stage. The piano-music faded to a roll of drums and the shrill cacophony of whistles as we cut in the sound-track of the film and a girl in a ballet-length evening gown stepped out under the full glare of the lights. She was of medium height, with black hair and a white, painted mask of a face. She was joined immediately by a heavy, balding man wearing the sober clothes of a bank manager. He turned her sideways on to the camera and she clasped her hands behind her head and stood in an attitude of wooden apathy as the man began to fumble with the back zip of her dress.

Against the background of the piano music I had been sketching in the main outlines of the Magdala's career for the benefit of the viewers. I timed it so that I finished speaking when the camera picked out the girl under the spotlights. I wanted us to cut it there but Kapper wouldn't hear of it.

"Get 'em all excited and take 'em in there and then not let them see anything, Cass?" he said. "What's got into you, boy? They'll be queueing up to get their licence money refunded if we don't let them have a little bit of fun."

So we stayed long enough to let the bank manager take off the girl's dress, and her slip, and make a start on the business of unfastening her brassière, and then cut abruptly to the studio interview.

The contrast was undeniably there. Whatever the viewers were expecting, Mary Magdala would surprise them.

She sat in the chair with an easy grace, her hands folded composedly in her lap. Tall and personable, with startlingly red hair and a strongly-boned face that was handsome rather than beautiful, she was wearing a loose-fitting coat and plain shoes. The coat was neither new, nor particularly stylish; an off-the-peg bargain picked up in a winter sale two, perhaps three, years before. But she wore it with distinction. Looking at her you knew instinctively that under the coat her figure was superb, and that she would walk like a thoroughbred. This much was obvious and in a curious way taken for granted. The large dark eyes, the flawless complexion, the casually-dressed red hair—these things were expected. What was astonishing was her serenity; a quality of bearing that wiped away the image of the girl being stripped in the cabaret with one magnificent, contemptuous stroke. Here was a woman of exceptional personality, who could sit still and silent in the corner of a crowded room and dominate it just by being there. It was impossible to think of her ever being embarrassed or off-balance. She did not react to other people; they reacted to her. In any group, on any occasion, she would be the catalyst, the initiator. I never remember seeing anyone so completely mistress of herself.

We brought her on to the screen in medium shot and dollied-in slowly, taking our time, giving the viewers an opportunity to look at her and catch the infection of her calm assurance. It was this deep untroubled poise which saved her from boldness, as the fine texture of her skin smoothed away any hint of coarseness from her face with its determined jaw-line and firmly-moulded nose. But what she had been like before she achieved serenity—the mental image of those long legs and that tossed red hair writhing and shaking under the staring lights of the cabaret stage—this was an electrifying thought.

"Miss Magdala," I said then, "thank you first of all for coming."

She nodded. "I'm glad to be there."

"It's very good of you."

This was throw-away stuff; pleasantries. But necessary pleasantries. I knew the viewers would need a moment or two to concentrate on what she was saying as well as on how she looked. She was my star witness and I wanted her to stay in their minds long after Pilate and Nicodemus had faded. But for the right reasons.

"The fact is," I said carefully, "we're trying to establish the truth about Jesus Davidson."

"Yes," she said, her voice low and clear.

There was nothing insipid about her. Whatever Davidson had done to change her he had not tamed nor diluted her spirit. I had met religious converts before—people who, in renouncing their former way of life, seemed also to have renounced life itself—and found them pathetically wan and colourless. The Magdala was not like that. She had seized whatever Davidson's gift had been—forgiveness, freedom—with both hands, as avidly as once she had embraced the career that had made her notorious. Looking at her you said to yourself not: "This is a beautiful woman," but: "This is a woman excitingly alive."

"I understand you knew him well?" I said.

"Yes."

"How well, Miss Magdala?"

"Very well."

"Intimately?" I chose the word deliberately.

She nodded. "Yes."

"I see."

She smiled at the tone of my voice, the corners of her mouth lifting, her eyebrows tilting a little. It was an amused, open smile with no hint of sophistry in it. I could imagine the effect it must have had on the audience when she was dancing.

"Surprised, Mr Tennel?"

"A little. You see, you are a. . . ."

"I know. I'm a cabaret-girl—or I was. And he is God."

"Something like that," I said.

She looked at me levelly. "You don't think God concerns himself with cabaret-girls, is that it?"

But I dodged that one. It was too early in the piece to let her ask the questions, especially theological ones.

"But is he God?" I said. "That's what we're trying to find out."

"Oh, yes," she said, and the confidence in her voice was a natural thing, as normal and unforced as the daylight. "He's God. The Blessed One. The Life of the world."

"Life?" I snatched at the word. "But we're talking about a dead man."

"I'm not. He was dead, certainly. But now he is alive again."

I nodded. "That's the rumour we've all heard, of course, but. . . ."

"Not a rumour," she said firmly. "The truth. You said you wanted the truth about him. Well, that's it. He's alive."

"You sound very sure of that, Miss Magdala."

"Very sure," she said.

"How can you be so sure?"

"Because I've seen him," she said simply.

Looking at her like this, in close-up, I felt the conviction in her voice come through with an almost physical impact. I dared to hope that even Patros would be disturbed by it.

However it was my job to break down her confidence if I could; to be as relentless with her as I had been with

Jacob Nicodemus. With her looks and background the line of attack was obvious.

"Miss Magdala," I said, "I can see you were very attached to him." I have had plenty of practice in this sort of thing and the implication of my words was clear enough.

But she disarmed me with one stroke.

"I love him, if that's what you mean," she said. She was looking directly into the camera lens and her words were like the declaration of a bride at her wedding.

"Yes," I said uncertainly. "Yes, I see."

I winced now, hearing my voice through the monitor speaker. I sounded as gauche as a schoolboy. I, Cass Tennel, who had reduced the most competent of actresses to embarrassed confusion in front of the camera; who had destroyed reputations for shrewdness and poise with a few carefully-chosen words. I, for whom nothing was sacred—not pain, not privacy, not grief—nothing. I sat and watched a Jewish cabaret-girl put me neatly in my place.

In my world people don't make declarations of love; at least, not after they have passed the age of ten. Love is not a word that comes easily, or indeed honestly, to our lips. Beyond the frontiers of childhood it is stripped of its innocence and becomes, at best, a polite synonym for sex. We use it self-consciously even in bed for we are no longer able to believe in its deeper implications of loyalty and tolerance. My generation 'wants' a woman, 'needs' a man. The need and the desire are physical; no more than that. We are adept at making love. But we are at once too immature and too sophisticated to be able to accept the reality of love as a gift to be given and received. Unable to surrender ourselves to it, we take the necessary precautions.

She looked at me and laughed. "You poor man. Now I've embarrassed you."

"No," I said. "It's just that. . . ."

"I don't mean that kind of loving," she said. "This is something quite different, although I suppose, in an odd sort of way, it grows out of human loving. But it's a new kind of love—the love he has set free in the world."

From anyone else it would have sounded intolerably mawkish. But the way she said it, and the excitement that quickened in her eyes, lifted the words into a new dimension. What she said was impressive. But it was not obviously meaningful. It was like asking an exceptional child to describe the world—half-real, half-dream—in which she lived. Something of the magic came through in the threadbare adult words. But the sensation I had was of standing just out of earshot, teased and stirred by something I couldn't quite get hold of.

I said. "I'm afraid that's a bit over my head, Miss Magdala."

"I know," she said ruefully. "I'm not very good at describing it yet. And it isn't going to be easy to get people to understand. He warned us about that. Desperate people—yes. People in trouble, facing a crisis. But not ordinary men and women with everything more or less under control. They're going to be the difficult ones. He found it hard enough himself to get through to them, let alone someone like me trying to do it."

"Perhaps if you could tell us something about him," I said. "The kind of person he was. Would you say he was a happy man, for instance?"

"Happy?" She tasted the word doubtfully. "No. Not really. It's not the sort of word you can use about him. It's too—vulnerable, if you see what I mean?"

"Well, no," I said. "I'm not quite. . . ."

"Like us," she said. "Trapped in a world too big for us to cope with. At the mercy of things outside our control. Happiness comes to people like us. And we try to hold on to it. But we can't. A word can destroy it, or a look. A letter or a telephone call or an accident involving a friend. Happiness is something we feel in spite of our circumstances, not because of them. It doesn't come often enough, and when it does come we can't enjoy it because we're afraid it'll be snatched away again." She smiled. "It wasn't like that with him. He wasn't trapped. He was free. Not a victim of circumstances but the master of them. In control—way above anything as chancy as happiness."

"You say he was in control. You mean before he died?"

"Even before he died. You know what his name means, don't you? Jesus—Jeshua—the Conqueror. That's the only way to describe him. He was a man who had won."

"But he didn't win. At the end, he was defeated."

She shook her head, the bright flame of her hair swinging. "No. That's what we thought. Last Friday afternoon that's the way it looked even to us. But now, everything's changed."

"Since yesterday morning?"

"Yes."

"I wonder if you could tell us what happened then, Miss Magdala? At the tomb, I mean."

"He broke out. Nothing they could do could hold him." She laughed, spreading her hands in a gesture of excitement. "They sealed up the tomb, you know, and mounted a guard. It was ridiculous. Pathetic. Like tying-up a sleeping lion with cotton thread. When he wakened he just snapped the thread and strode out."

I found myself thinking that if this cult of Davidson caught on one of its biggest problems would be to overcome this kind of naïve and rather fulsome imagery. I could imagine how third-rate poets would go to work on something as incredible as a resurrection.

But on her lips the words once again discovered a certain dignity. From her, at least in the moment of speaking, it was artless and convincing.

"You say you saw him there, outside the tomb?"

"I did indeed."

"Alive?"

"Of course."

"Miss Magdala," I said brutally, "I'm sorry, but that's just not possible."

She was quite unshaken. "It's a miracle, Mr Tennel. They come naturally to him, of course. I'm ashamed to think how slow we've been to recognize this."

"It's understandable," I said. "I'm not much for miracles myself."

"He performed many, Mr Tennel. A great many."

"So I'm told."

"The trouble is, people misunderstood them."

"Didn't believe in them, you mean?"

"Oh no. They believed all right. If you see a cripple get up and walk, and listen to a deaf-mute you've known all your life suddenly start singing, you haven't much option, have you? When it happens like that, in front of a crowd, you've got to believe it." She shook her head again—that gesture of mingled frustration and excitement I was beginning to associate with people who had known Davidson. "It was the meaning of what he did they couldn't understand. They thought he was just a man doing something extraordinary."

"Yes," I said.

"No. That's exactly the point. He wasn't an ordinary man. He was God. God in person, doing the things that came naturally to him. People always said, 'How can this village nobody work miracles?' But the real question is, 'How can God walk about Israel like a man?' That's the basic miracle, Mr Tennel, that he was here at all. Once you've seen that, the rest is perfectly logical.''

"Even a resurrection?"

"Especially that. Death can't hold God."

Neither Nicodemus nor Thomas Didymus had dared to say that. "God can't die" was the brick wall beyond which they could not go. But "Death can't hold God" was the statement of a woman on the other side of that wall. A woman living in a new dimension, beyond the fear of death. This was the secret of her assurance; the absolute security upon which she stood serene. I looked at her with sudden compassion, remembering the tortured eyes of Thomas Didymus. She was facing an appalling personal disaster if one day, for her also, the dream should wither and die.

I said, "And you saw him there, in the garden outside the tomb?"

"That's right. I saw him and talked to him." I heard the patience in her voice and smiled, watching the screen. She was right, of course. Once you had swallowed the incredible idea of God living in the world as a man, everything else was completely logical. But it wasn't the enervating logic of the scholars; the logic that begins with the primary fact of birth and traces the course of life through growth and decline to the oblivion of the grave. This was a new kind of logic. A liberating logic that began fearlessly with the fact of death and argued its way into life. In the context of that logic my harping on the physical phenomenon of the re-appearance of Davidson was irritatingly naïve.

I began to understand why the word freedom kept cropping up in my conversations with these people who had known him. I saw it for the first time as being a religious, not a political, word. But what kind of a religion was this that took the moral issues of good and evil as read and concentrated on freedom and love? That eluded the intellectual grasp of a priest and was yet understood by a cabaret dancer?

I said, "How did you come to be in the garden so early in the morning? Was it pre-arranged before he died? A sort of rendezvous?"

She laughed. "Nothing so dramatic. It was simply our first opportunity to visit his tomb. We have a strict rule about not working on the Sabbath, as I expect you know. We had to wait until first light yesterday before we could go."

"Yes, but why did you go? Was it just a sentimental journey?"

"In a way, I suppose it was," she said frankly. "But practical too. We took spices and ointment and—oh, it sounds absurd now, a bunch of women in heavy mourning going to preserve a corpse. But it was all we could think of doing. We'd had to stand by and watch them take him away and kill him. And the burial on Friday was very rushed. We had to get finished before the Sabbath started at sunset. Yesterday morning we decided to do things properly. Give him a decent burial at least." She smiled. "I expect it all sounds very odd to you, Mr Tennel. But our Jewish funeral customs are important to us."

"I understand," I said.

"We were terribly worried about how we were going to get into the tomb—what with that great stone slab sealing the entrance and the guard there and everything. But of course, when we got there, the guards had gone and the tomb was wide open. And when we looked inside, it was empty."

I nodded. This was familiar ground by now. "You've considered the possibility of grave-robbers?"

"It was our first thought. I remember Salome—she was one of the group—saying in that rather acid voice she puts on when she's upset, 'Even when the poor soul's dead they can't leave him in peace.' "

I looked at her quickly. "They?"

"The Sanhedrin."

"You thought the Sanhedrin had arranged to have the body removed?"

"Yes, of course. Who else would want to do such a thing?"

"Why the Sanhedrin?" I said.

"I don't know. Perhaps to prevent the tomb from becoming a shrine. If it hadn't been for Saul Joseph offering his own tomb they'd have buried him in quick-lime in the prison yard. That's what usually happens."

"I wondered about that."

She nodded. "Mr Joseph went personally to the Governor-General and got his permission to bury the body. The Sanhedrin were very put out about it, I believe."

I could understand their alarm. A dead hero in a magnificent tomb was a ready-made focal point for future trouble.

"But it wasn't that at all, of course," she said. "We rushed back to the house and told the men. And John Zebedee and Peter Johnson went back straightaway to see for themselves. I followed behind but I hadn't a hope of catching up with them."

I said, "I'd like to get this quite right. It's important, I think. Are you in fact saying that the men were surprised at your news of the empty tomb?"

"And angry. Peter especially. I've never seen him so wild."

"It would be true to say, then, that these men who were his closest friends never expected him to come back from the dead?"

"None of us did, Mr Tennel. None of us."

"Although he had on several occasions promised to do just that?"

"In spite of that we didn't expect to see him alive again. I'm ashamed to have to say it, but it's true."

"And the men had been with you right through from Friday evening?"

"Yes."

"Thank you," I said. "Please go on. What happened when you got to the tomb the second time?"

"I saw Peter coming out. I hardly recognized him, he looked so old and beaten. John took his arm and they went off together, walking slowly. They passed right by me but I don't think either of them knew I was there. They were like men walking in their sleep."

"And did you go after them?"

"No. I stayed on. I don't know why. I was weeping and terribly upset, and ..."

"I quite understand, Miss Magdala. This has all been a tremendous strain on you."

She looked at me steadily and said, "You don't believe it, do you? You don't believe he's alive again?"

"I'm open to conviction," I said.

She shook her head. "You think I'm not quite myself. A little bit off-centre. You think it's all been too much of a shock for me. Well, it was a shock, finding that empty tomb. A terrible shock."

"Yes," I said. "Of course."

"The thought of them mauling him about. Dragging

him out of his grave in the middle of the night and digging a hole somewhere and dropping his body in and stamping the ground down on top of him. Just for a moment or two, there by myself in the garden when the men had gone, I thought I was going out of my mind." She smiled, a warm, sane smile. "And then he came and spoke to me."

"Jesus Davidson? You're sure?"

"Yes. He was suddenly there and he asked me why I was crying. He sounded so—so normal and relaxed I didn't think it was him at first. Funny isn't it, the way a familiar voice sounds strange when you don't expect to hear it? But then he spoke my name. 'Mary' he said. And I knew who he was and turned round and saw him there."

Again it was said with that devastating simplicity, as though she had wakened from a nightmare and recognized the familiar room and the figure of a parent bending over her. Watching her and listening to her voice was like living through a Greek tragedy of great power and realism and then finding a fairy-story, happy-ever-after ending grafted on to the last act. As a climax it was an insult to the intelligence of the audience. And yet, unless that fairy-story ending of a dead man come back to life could be accepted as being as real and credible as the first part of the tragedy, then the whole piece was meaningless nonsense and the hero of it absurd.

"Did he say anything else?" I said.

"He gave me a message. For Peter and the men. He called them his brothers. I put my arms round him and hugged him. He was there and I was so glad to see him, and at the same time terrified in case he disappeared again. I held him tight to make sure of him. But he freed himself gently and told me to take this message back to the house."

"What was the message? Can you tell us?"

"Oh yes. It's not a secret. We're finished with secrets now. It's all out in the open for everyone to hear. I mean, if killing him couldn't silence him, nothing can. He said, 'Go and tell my brothers I am ascending to my Father and yours, to my God and your God. Tell them I am going first to Galilee and they must come and meet me there.'"

"And you took that message back to them?"

She nodded. "I ran all the way. I was so excited I could hardly get the words out at first."

"Did they understand what he meant, Miss Magdala?"

"Yes. It was exactly what he had promised. He told us all about it long before any of this happened; how he came from God and was going back to God. He told us plainly, not once but many times."

"And yet at first, when you found the tomb empty, you didn't even consider the possibility of a resurrection."

"I know," she said. "He told us exactly what would happen, and we wanted to believe him, but I don't think any of us really expected it to come true." She shook her head. "Looking back now over the last couple of years I think we must have broken his heart a hundred times simply by not being able to understand the truth about him and what he was trying to do for us."

I remembered how Thomas Didymus had said much the same thing; the failure of faith that had destroyed Jesus Davidson. For him it had become the ultimate failure. But not for Mary Magdala.

"Have the men gone north?" I said.

She nodded.

"And you? When will you go?"

"Soon. Tomorrow perhaps. Or the day after."

I said. "That's where it all began, isn't it? In Galilee."

"Yes."

"Is that where you first met him, Miss Magdala?"

"Yes. In Tiberias. I was run-down and nervy. I'd been working too hard in the cabarets." She looked at me calmly. "Not the easiest kind of work, Mr Tennel, as you can imagine. The doctor ordered a complete rest. You know the sort of thing—country air, regular meals, plenty of early nights. I went up to a little place by the lake. Right off the map and as quiet as a church." She shrugged her shoulders and smiled. "It sounded ideal, but after a couple of weeks of it I wasn't the slightest bit better. Worse, if anything. Depressed, no appetite, sleeping badly. I'd got to the stage where I just wasn't interested in living. The countryside was beautiful and everyone was very kind. But it was all remote somehow— out of my reach. I was there, in the middle of it, but I wasn't a part of it. I felt like a ghost.

"The doctor said it was all tied up with my life in the cabarets. Too many nights on the stage, with all those eyes watching me out of the darkness. You can't see them, you know—the spotlights take care of that. But you can feel them. It's not the pleasantest of feelings. You're on your own up there under the lights in an intense little private world. Only it isn't really private. It's like being under a microscope. After a time you begin to lose your sense of reality.

"I expect it sounds ridiculous to you, Mr Tennel, but it had me scared. Really scared."

I nodded. "And then you met Davidson."

"Yes. I didn't want to go. I didn't want to see anyone. I just wasn't interested. But they insisted. He'd got a reputation for being able to help people and they felt it was worth a try."

"What happened," I said, "when you met him?"

She looked faintly surprised. "He cured me."

"You mean he gave you treatment? Some sort of therapy?"

She shook her head. "It's no good, Mr Tennel. You mustn't try to fit him into some sort of recognized category—a kind of super-psychiatrist or something. When I say he cured me, I mean just that. They brought me to him, and he set me free."

Free. That same word again. They all used it, simply, without explanations; as though, once it was spoken, everything had been explained.

I said cautiously, remembering Zaccheus, "You mean he forgave you?"

"Of course. He forgave me, he set me free, he cured me—they all mean the same thing, Mr Tennel. They all add up to life."

Here we go again, I thought, Metaphysics for the masses.

"He accepted me as I was," she said. "As a person. It'd been a long time since anyone'd done that."

"I find that hard to credit," I said. "You were famous as a dancer. Everyone in Jerusalem knew the Magdala."

"The Magdala," she said, the sharpness of contempt in her voice. "A dancer. A name on a poster. A body posturing under the lights when the drums began to beat. But I'm a person, Mr Tennel. A human being needing people, needing love. And that's how he accepted me; as a woman capable of going out of her mind."

I said, "But the people you were staying with in Galilee —surely they accepted you as a person too?"

She smiled. "They were very kind to me."

"That's something," I said. "To be kind to people in trouble."

"Oh, I was grateful, Mr Tennel. They did all they could to help me. But it wasn't enough. Nothing like enough. It never is. You know that."

I knew that. Everyone does. Kindness can sometimes prevent a tragedy. But once the tragedy has happened kindness—the best that is in us—is hopelessly inadequate. It can cushion but it can't cure.

"And yet," I said, "when this man accepted you. . . ."

"That's different, isn't it?"

"How?"

"Because he's God," she said. "Only God is strong enough to go beyond kindness; to accept us as we are and make us whole again."

"But what exactly did he do?" I said. "If you could give us some idea. . . ."

"I know," she said. "I know what you want me to say. Shock treatment, injections, the clinical mystery of the consulting-room that makes everything credible."

"Well," I said uncomfortably, "you must admit it would. . ."

She broke in crisply, "The truth is, Mr Tennel, he didn't do anything—not in the sense you mean. He looked at me and spoke my name. He didn't even touch me. But I felt suddenly light and empty and I thought I was going to faint. And then I was weeping, and all the strain was washing away, and I felt everything coming back into focus around me—the houses and the grass and the trees —they sort of grew up and made a place for me to stand. And the faces of my friends were clear and alive, and I heard them talking and the sounds of the town all round me. I wasn't a ghost any more. I was alive, part of the world a person in my own right.

"It was a little resurrection," she said. "I understand that now. Like being born again."

"And all this happened," I said carefully, "because you trusted him?"

"Yes. That's exactly right. Because I trusted him."

"Miss Magdala," I said, "I'm not at all sure that I understand all of that. But this much I do understand— the sort of person you have become—your peace of mind, your happiness, indeed your basic ability to go on living —all this depends, it seems to me, on one vital fact—that Jesus Davidson was what he claimed to be."

She nodded happily. "Yes, Mr Tennel. Because he is who he is, I am who I am."

"And would it be true to say that unless he is alive now there can be no life for you?"

"For me or for any of us."

I nodded, letting that pass. "So it is very important to you that you saw him in the garden yesterday morning."

"Of course."

I said, "Have you seen him since?"

"Not yet. But some of the others have."

I smiled at her. "Miss Magdala, we're most grateful to you. You've made it all vivid and . . ."

"Believable?" she said quickly, matching me smile for smile.

I hesitated. "Worth thinking about, anyway."

I took my cue and turned to Number One camera.

"I think you'll agree that's a remarkable story. And a very moving one. Whether or not it's true is another matter.

"Not that anyone here doubts the sincerity of Miss Magdala. It is transparently clear that she believes she has seen Jesus Davidson alive after his death and spoken to him. And the implications of this are very great indeed.

"At the same time," I said, "Miss Magdala is a sensitive and highly-strung person who has had what amounts to a nervous breakdown and who witnessed, as recently as last Friday, the execution of a young man to whom she was—

at the very least—deeply attached. On her own admission she was alone at the tomb when she claims to have seen and heard the resurrected man. She says other people have seen him since then, and this may be true. But until we have heard further evidence we must, in fairness to her, keep an open mind."

This was my escape clause, my little bit of insurance against Patros's reaction. Kapper had insisted I put it in.

"It's different for you, Cass," he said. "You're here, right in the middle of it. You've been chasing round talking to people for the last thirty-six hours and you're tired and nervy. It's all happened too quickly and you haven't had a chance to digest it." He smiled, not unkindly. "Besides, she's a very attractive woman."

"That's got nothing to do with it," I said.

"Perhaps not, but it helps. Whether or not you believe Davidson's alive again, any fool watching you in that interview will know one thing for sure. You're sold on the Magdala. Utterly and completely. You believe every word she says."

I opened my mouth to protest but he cut me short. "Oh, I don't blame you, Cass. She's quite a woman, and very persuasive. Especially when she's sitting there in front of you. And that's the point, d'you see? It's not going to be like that for Patros. He'll be sitting in front of a screen in Rome watching it all in black and white and two dimensions. Maybe it'll get through to him. Maybe it won't. That's why we've got to take precautions."

"Didn't she convince you?" I said'

But he refused to be drawn. "It's not me, Cass. It's Patros."

"But. . . ."

"Look, we've both put our heads on the block with

this story, Cass. Let's at least do what we can to make it comfortable."

"There's no doubt about one thing," I said now to the camera. "The tomb was empty yesterday morning and the body of Davidson is missing. Everyone is agreed about that. To discover the official religious view of this event we went this afternoon to see His Grace the High Priest. . . ."

10

Since the meeting of the Sanhedrin on Sunday Kapper's secretary had made a number of unsuccessful attempts to fix an appointment for me with the High Priest. Just before eleven on the Monday morning she reported yet another failure.

"I'm sorry, Mr Tennel," she said. "I can't get past the switchboard. Always the same answer—'His Grace is not receiving calls at the moment.'"

At Kapper's suggestion I picked up the phone to see if I could break through the barrier. The girl on the switchboard in the Palace gave me the answer she had given Kapper's secretary but I refused to accept it. I explained who I was and dropped a few important names and bullied her a little, and after some hesitation she put me through to his chaplain.

"An interview with His Grace?" he said. "Quite impossible, I'm afraid." It was the voice of a youngish man, cultured, smooth, adept at closing doors. I took an instant dislike to him. "His Grace is not receiving. . . ."

". . . calls at the moment," I finished it for him. "Yes, I know. But this is urgent."

"I'm so sorry," he said. "No."

"When will he be available?"

"Hard to say. Later in the week, perhaps. More likely

next week. We have just had a major religious festival and. . . ."

"I'm well aware of that."

Some of the smoothness rubbed off his voice. "Then you are perhaps also aware of the fact that His Grace is extremely tired. Very considerable demands have been made upon his time and energies over the last few days. It is essential that he be allowed to rest now."

"We all have demands made upon us, Rabbi," I said. "Life is a demanding occupation. It is vitally important that I talk to Lord Caiaphas today."

"I repeat, quite impossible."

I said, "I wonder if you appreciate just how important it is?"

"To you, possibly," he said. "We all consider our particular job to be supremely significant."

I controlled myself with an effort. "Not only to me. I should've thought it obvious that it is important to the Jewish community as a whole, and to Lord Caiaphas personally, that an authoritative statement on behalf of the Church should be included in my programme to-night. His Excellency the Governor-General has been very willing to speak about the political implications of this rumour about Jesus Davidson. It will look a little odd, don't you think, if the High Priest refuses to co-operate?"

He said, "It's not a question of refusing to co-operate, Mr Tennel. As I have already told you, His Grace is exhausted. As a layman you cannot imagine the strain an occasion of this nature puts upon him."

"You mean, the Festival?"

"Naturally."

"He's too tired to talk?"

"Put bluntly, that is correct."

"I don't think so," I said. "If we're going to be blunt it's not a question of fatigue, it's a question of fear."

There was a moment or two of silence and then he said, "That suggestion is both infamous and absurd."

"Perhaps. But it makes sense to me, Rabbi, as your excuses about fatigue quite frankly don't."

"Mr Tennel, if you had ever met His Grace you would realize just how ridiculous your suggestion is. The High Priest of Jewry fears no man. He fears only God."

"My point precisely," I said.

He hesitated. "I'm afraid I don't quite. . . ."

"Look, Rabbi. I've been in Jerusalem a little over twenty-four hours. During that time it's become clear to me that in the opinion of a great many people Jesus Davidson is God."

"You cannot expect me," he said stiffly, "to listen to blasphemy even from one who is outside our Faith."

I said, "You mean the idea frightens you too?"

"Davidson is dead." I detected a note of uncertainty like a snagged thread in the smoothness of his voice. "It is not our custom to fear the dead, Mr Tennel, whoever they may have been."

"Of course," I said. "Provided they stay dead. But what if they don't? What if a man who died last Friday afternoon was seen walking about alive yesterday morning? Isn't it just possible that even your High Priest might be a little afraid of a man like that?"

"You're talking nonsense, Mr Tennel, if I may say so. Irresponsible nonsense."

"You think Davidson is still dead?"

"Of course."

"That's the official view in the Palace, is it?"

"Certainly."

"I see. Then for the life of me I can't understand why His Grace refuses to sit in front of one of our cameras and say so."

I heard him draw in his breath in annoyance. "I can only reiterate that His Grace is. . . ."

"Tired. Yes, I know. And so am I, Rabbi. Tired of evasive tactics in high places. I think you are probably wise to be so afraid of Jesus Davidson, but I'm a little shattered that you make it so obvious. Tell His Grace that my programme goes out at nine tonight. Tell him we're using the WTA link. That's world coverage, Rabbi. Impress that fact on him, will you? World coverage. And tell him one more thing—if he refuses to appear on the programme we'll feel free to draw our own conclusions and share them with the viewers. They won't necessarily be complimentary."

"Mr Tennel," he said, worried now but still game; still doing his diplomatic stuff, "I don't know what you hope to achieve by these methods, but let me assure you that we are not. . . ."

"Goodbye, Rabbi," I said gently, and put the phone down.

He rang back within the hour. His voice had recovered its full smooth flavour. He said that His Grace would be happy to grant us an interview. Two o'clock at the Palace, and would we please endeavour to be puntual. I said we would.

Finely-boned and ascetic above the neatly-trimmed beard, the face of Caiaphas, High Priest of Jewry, looked at me dispassionately from the monitor screen. There was breeding in the high forehead, the firmly-chiselled nose. From under arched brows his eyes watched the world, as black and as cold as the eyes of a snake.

"Lord Caiaphas," I heard my voice say, "perhaps we

may begin with the special meeting of the Sanhedrin yesterday morning?"

He inclined his head gravely. "As you wish." In his formal silk cassock, a small skull-cap on his head, he sat relaxed and yet alert, the book-lined wall of his study behind him.

He had been sitting in exactly this position when we walked into the room that afternoon. The study itself had been designed not so much to induce contemplative thought as to intimidate visitors. The books on the shelves, the pattern in the carpet, the carefully calculated angles at which the chairs were set—all this had drawn our eyes to Caiaphas. He sat, as it were, in the centre of a magnetic field; a man who compelled attention not because his was an attractive personality but because he was dangerous. The sense of danger emanated from him like an electric current. Watching him now on the monitor I remembered how we had paused in the doorway, intensely aware of that seated figure, and how Greg had murmured in my ear, "Careful, Cass. This one bites."

"Would you care to tell us what it was about?" I said.

He shrugged. "It was concerned with the blasphemer Davidson."

"A sort of post-mortem?"

"If you like."

I nodded. "Is it true that you pressed for his execution in the Sanhedrin last Thursday night?"

"It was my duty to do so, Mr Tennel."

"And that you went personally to the Governor-General to obtain his sanction for the verdict?"

"Quite true. He was, I am happy to say, most co-operative and helpful."

I left that for Pilate to pick up and cherish if he wished.

"Why?" I said. "Why was it so important to you that he should die?"

His arched brows lifted. "Not to me personally. I am a priest of God, Mr Tennel. As such I desire the death of no man. But as High Priest of Jewry I have certain responsibilities. In the interests of our nation it was essential that he should die."

He looked unblinkingly at the camera, the words coming dry and colourless from his lips. We might have been discussing the uprooting of an unproductive vine.

"But surely, Your Grace, he did a great deal for the nation? At least at the grass-roots level of the ordinary people. His healing, for instance, and his reputation for. . . ."

"He was a religious charlatan, Mr Tennel." His voice sliced into my sentence, coldly surgical rather than angry. "A heretic and a rabble-rouser. We cannot afford such men in Jewry."

I said, "There was a political angle too, wasn't there?"

"There is always a political angle." The thin lips stretched briefly indicating amusement. "That is something Rome has taught us all."

"Would you care to comment on the political aspect of the case?"

"I don't think so. I imagine His Excellency the Governor-General has fully covered that."

Kapper had warned me he would be difficult to shake. After the nervousness of Pilate there was something impressive about his cold authority. He handled my questions with an almost contemptuous calm, choosing his words unhurriedly, refusing to be drawn.

"To get back to yesterday's meeting," I said. "Did you discuss this rumour about his resurrection?"

He looked at me sourly. "We are not in the habit of convening the Sanhedrin to waste the members' time discussing rumours. Our interest is in facts."

"But it is a fact, isn't it, that Davidson's tomb was found empty yesterday morning?"

"Indeed." He bit off the word with an expression of bored distaste.

"What did the Sanhedrin make of that, Your Grace?"

"A simple, if rather clumsy, case of grave-robbing. Some of his gang broke into the tomb in the night and stole the body."

"I see."

"We were expecting it, of course."

"Oh?"

He sighed. "He had been reckless enough, on more than one occasion, to predict his own resurrection."

"But surely stealing a body can hardly be described as a resurrection."

"It can be made to look very like one, Mr Tennel."

"I suppose so." I paused for just a moment and then said, "What about the earthquake?"

"I know nothing of that," he said, a shade quickly. "I certainly felt no earthquake. Nor, I understand, did His Excellency"

"So he told me."

I waited a little longer this time.

"I'm afraid some of our people are a little—imaginative," he said then. "Signs and portents. You know the sort of thing."

"Like the way the Temple curtain tore down the middle at the moment of his death last Friday?"

"Oh," he said, curling his lip, "that."

I nodded. "Odd, wasn't it?"

"It was despicable," he said. "An act of vandalism."

"You think someone sneaked in and deliberately ripped it?"

"Of course. One of the gang. It's the obvious explanation. Those ignorant louts he gathered round him. . . ." He compressed his lips, his eyes hard. "It's all of a piece with his inflammatory speeches and his fake miracles. The man was a crude exhibitionist playing on the emotions of gullible fools. The Galilean towns are rife with absurd legends about him—walking on the lake, conjuring up shoals of fish, feeding five thousand people with a handful of food. Gimmicks, Mr Tennel. Disgusting, blasphemous gimmicks."

I switched him back abruptly. "I understand the guards were overpowered—at the tomb, I mean."

He gave me an angry little smile, his teeth showing small and white against his beard. "Ah yes, the guards. I hoped you would spare me that, Mr Tennel. A very tender spot, I fear."

"They were outnumbered, of course?"

He looked at me and shook his head. "I can see we must make a clean breast of it, Mr Tennel. They were not outnumbered. The fact is, they were asleep. And while they slept, the tomb was robbed."

This really shook me. I had expected him to be ruthless in his attempt to destroy the image of the man whom he had manœuvred Pilate into executing, but not so ruthless as this.

"A painful admission, I'm afraid," he said coolly. "And a damaging one to Jewish military pride. But there it is. Truth will out, Mr Tennel. We may not be very good soldiers but at least we can be honest men."

Try telling that to Major Sanballet, I thought. And wondered what remote, dead-end posting had been chosen for him since yesterday morning.

I said, "It's hard to credit they were all asleep, Your Grace. One or two, perhaps. But the whole contingent. . . ."

He twitched his lips. "You press me hard, Mr Tennel."

"I'd like an answer."

He nodded. "Shall we just say that it is not unusual for there to be a certain amount of injudicious—well, celebration, at the end of a Festival Sabbath? I'm not in any way seeking to make excuses. But the men had been under considerable pressure during the week, and when the Sabbath ended at six o'clock on Saturday evening. . . ."

"A drunken stupor," I said bluntly. "Is that what you're implying?"

He shrugged and spread his hands. "A most unfortunate lapse."

"But understandable," I said.

"You're very kind."

"And plausible too, as excuses go."

His eyes blazed. But before he could speak I said, "Summing-up so far, then, the main points seem to be: Davidson was properly executed and his body buried in a tomb. Sometime on Saturday night or very early Sunday morning, whilst the guards were—shall we say incapacitated?—the tomb was broken into and the body stolen. Is that right?"

"Perfectly correct. A succinct summary of the official statement we have issued to the Press for tomorrow's editions."

"That means it's the official view of the Church?"

"It is."

I smiled. "Then, Your Grace, what would you say if I told you that we have evidence that Jesus Davidson has been seen alive in the last twenty-four hours? And that he has spoken to someone?"

"Nonsense," he said contemptuously. "That is what I should say. Nonsense. And vicious, irresponsible nonsense at that."

"It sounded neither vicious nor irresponsible to us," I said gently.

He pursed his lips. "Mr Tennel, I see I must be frank with you. We have had a great deal of trouble with Davidson. I think I may say with justice that we have been extremely patient and lenient in the matter. . . ."

"Lenient, Your Grace? But you had him executed."

"Only as a last resort. Only because he left us with no alternative. He has had the run of the country for three years. We could have had him arrested at any time during that period. He certainly gave us cause enough. During the whole of that time he showed nothing but antagonism towards the established Church. Indeed, he went out of his way to be deliberately abusive to some of our most distinguished scholars, and lost no opportunity of undermining our authority and the good standing of the true Faith."

I said, "But couldn't that be said, in fact, of every great reformer?"

"A village joiner who sits drinking in taverns and chooses his friends from the lowest strata of our society can hardly be described as a religious reformer, Mr Tennel." He leaned forward, hunching his shoulders. "I wonder if you realize how delicate our position is in this country today? We are a proud people who do not take kindly to occupation by a foreign power. I think it is fair to say that the peace and welfare of the nation can only be sustained by the existence of a strong Church. Once the authority of the Church is questioned we could quickly come to disaster. That is why, in the end, we had to take decisive action against Davidson. Another year—

eighteen months at the most—and he would have destroyed the moral fibre of our people with his teaching; the complex code of public and private morality which is the outward expression of our deep spiritual convictions. This is what he attacked, Mr Tennel, the law of God by which we order our lives and in the strength of which we have been able to retain our national identity in the face of repeated invasions and occupations by our enemies.

"We are an intensely religious people, Mr Tennel, struggling to hold our place in a world which has, in the main, grown tired of religion. We are not unaware of the fact that in the eyes of that world much of what we do is considered trivial—even absurd. Our insistence on the sanctity of our Law which provides correct procedures for the carrying out of every task, from the simplest routines of the housewife in her kitchen to the major ceremonial occasions in the Temple—we know that this is regarded by many people as a tangled web of superstition. Our Sabbath observance which takes precedence over every emergency, our professional holy men—the Pharisees— whose vocation it is to perform the minutiae of the Law in public places so that all men may observe their actions and be chastened, our faithful commemoration of the great historical events by means of which God has made himself known to us, our unleavened bread, our strict diet, our phylacteries—we know that these are objects of amusement to our neighbours in other countries. But they are meaningful to us and we have proved their worth. Our security is rooted in them.

"We are a small nation, Mr Tennel, and our neighbours have always been far more powerful than we. And yet we have outlived them all. Egypt, Persia, Greece—we have seen them all go down whilst we ourselves have survived uncorrupted. Not because we are stronger than they, but because we have remained faithful to God's law.

"That is why we had to silence Davidson. He broke the law continually, and he encouraged our people to break it. Indeed, he taught openly that only by breaking the law could men truly honour God. I hope I have said sufficient to convince you of the appalling consequences which could follow the embracing of so reckless a philosophy." He leaned back in his chair then, shaking his head slowly, that wintry smile lifting his mouth but failing to reach his eyes. "He was not a reformer, Mr Tennel, he was a revolutionary. Fortunately for us, not a very skilled one."

No match for you, anyway, my friend, I thought.

I said, "It is expedient that one man should die, and the country be saved."

He nodded. "Exactly. That is the whole point. If you understand that, you will understand how little can we afford now to have wild rumours of his resurrection bandied about the streets. Jesus Davidson is dead. That is a fact, Mr Tennel. If I may be permitted a small touch of humour to lighten this somewhat lugubrious atmosphere of tension, it is not only a fact, it is a cold fact."

I looked at him with dislike. "I find your humour a little grim, Your Grace."

"Possibly, possibly. But harmless, Mr Tennel, I think. Which is more than can be said for this wicked lie about resurrection."

Urbane and confident, his voice flicked like a glove across my face. I felt my temper rising and forced myself to speak quietly.

"They say he claimed to be Messiah."

"He made many claims, but the sharp reality of the gallows disproved them all. You cannot bluff death, Mr Tennel."

136

His constant use of my name was deliberately irritating. I recognized the technique; it was one I had often used myself. It did nothing to endear him to me.

"No," I said. "But is it perhaps possible that in Jesus Davidson we have found a man who can overcome death? Who possesses the ultimate Messianic gift—the power to lay down his life, and the power to take it up again?"

He looked at me with narrowed eyes. "I am flattered to discover that you have made some study of our faith, Mr Tennel. I had, quite frankly, not expected such erudition in a Gentile." He joined the tops of his fingers together and stroked his beard with his thumbs. "I have no wish to appear pedantic," he said, looking the epitome of pedantry, "but your information is not entirely accurate. Power over death is certainly a Messianic characteristic. But your interpretation of it is erroneous. Messiah is stronger than death. Which means, quite simply, that he cannot die. If we had had any doubts about the identity of Davidson, his death last Friday afternoon would have dispelled them completely."

I said, "Did you, in fact, have any doubts about him?"

"No, we did not."

"You never, at any time, suspected that he might be Messiah?"

"Not for one moment."

"Many people did, Your Grace."

I saw the flicker of annoyance in his eyes. "The world is full of foolish men who are all too easily led astray, Mr Tennel. Men who will believe anything—however absurd —if it is told them often enough."

I nodded. "I agree. But I'm speaking now of intelligent people—men and women with plenty of common-sense, who began by being sceptical of his claims and became, in the end, his devoted followers."

"It is my experience," he said smoothly, "that many otherwise intelligent people tend to be inexplicably naïve in matters of religion. I should have thought, Mr Tennel, that you would accept the judgement of a professional theologian rather than the wishful thinking of those who have had no specific training in spiritual understanding. I can assure you that when Messiah comes, we who have devoted our lives to the study of God's Law will be the first to recognize and acclaim him."

"Yes, of course," I said.

He was pleased to have his point accepted. For the first time there was just a touch of warmth in his smile. "We gave him every possible opportunity to substantiate his claims, you know. Even at his trial last Thursday night, when the evidence against him was so massively conclusive, we went out of our way to enable him to give us some clear indication that he was who he claimed to be."

"You invited him to declare himself?"

"We did."

"What did he say?"

The smile faded, leaving his face cold and hard. "He used the secret name of God."

"I'm sorry," I said, "I'm afraid I don't quite. . . ?"

"The forbidden name—the holy name—to be spoken only by the High Priest in the secret place of the Temple."

"Behind the great curtain?"

He nodded. "Just so. It is the name God gave to Moses in the desert. The name that was to set our people free from the slavery of Egypt. Since that day for a man to use it casually has been a sin in our eyes. For a man to use it of himself—the ultimate, unthinkable blasphemy."

"And this is what Davidson did at his trial?"

"Yes." Pale and shocked, his face filled the screen.

I said, "He called himself God?"

"He did."

"And because he called himself God, he had to die?"

"The ultimate blasphemy, Mr Tennel. We had no alternative."

"No," I said carefully, "I suppose not. And yet—forgive me, Your Grace—but it seems to me that if he was Messiah then he also had no alternative. I mean, you asked him to declare himself, and that's what he did, surely?"

He seemed to withdraw into himself, his head sinking into his shoulders, his eyes watching me behind half-closed lids.

"Are you suggesting that we. . . ?"

"I'm not suggesting anything, Your Grace," I said gently. "It just seems odd to me that a man on trial for his life should be deliberately invited to condemn himself."

He said sharply, "That is a gross misrepresentation of the facts."

"I'm sorry, Your Grace. But you must admit that to somebody not conversant with your legal procedure it looks uncommonly like. . . ."

"I admit nothing." His voice was ruffled now, edgy with anger and just a trace of fear. "If he had been Messiah do you think for one moment it would ever have come to that? To a trial for his life before the highest ecclesiastical court in the land?"

"I suppose not."

"Unthinkable, Mr Tennel. Quite unthinkable. When Messiah comes he will be clothed in power and majesty. The whole world will bow to his will and his glory will encompass mankind." The words took hold of him, lifting his voice into that curious chanting which Nicodemus had used. "His rising will be like the sun at noon and none shall be able to withstand him. His cloak shall be the canopy of heaven, and the earth his footstool. The islands will rejoice at his coming and the little hills clap their hands for joy." He stopped abruptly and looked at me malevolently, his eyes like black glass in the pallor of his face. "The man we executed for blasphemy and treason was not like that, Mr Tennel. He was shabby and poor. A Nazarene and a drunkard. Not for him the companionship of the heavenly host. His friends were vagabonds and malcontents, the dregs of our nation. His words were words of folly, not of wisdom, and his end, like his beginning, was without dignity."

"The caterpillar and the butterfly," I said slowly.

"I beg your pardon, Mr Tennel?"

"I'm sorry, Your Grace. I was just thinking aloud."

"Indeed?" He raised his brows sardonically. "About butterflies?"

I said, "You know that story that keeps cropping up in the history of every nation, Your Grace? The one about the king who disguises himself as a commoner and moves unrecognized among the people. Suppose there is a God who decided to do just that. Theology is not my subject, of course, but. . . ."

"I'm glad to hear you confess it, Mr Tennel."

"All right," I said, smiling. "But suppose it's true that God cares about us. About ordinary people. Really cares, I mean. Enough to become one of us. To be born; to share in the life we know—the tears, the pain, the disappointments. To put on one side his glory; strip off his majesty; suffer with his people. And in the end, die."

"I must protest, Mr Tennel. Even as an excursion into fantasy this is quite preposterous."

"Die on a gallows," I said, "and be buried in a tomb. And then, break out into life again. Reveal himself in his true colours. All that imagery you've been using about the true Messiah, Your Grace—the power and the glory—all that rising into new life like the brilliance of the butterfly emerging from the embalmed body of the drab little caterpillar." I waited, watching him. Greg had him in close-up and I could see the struggle of emotions going on behind the smooth disdain of his expression. Anger and fear and doubt all fighting together, and his superb control mastering them one by one. Only the fine mist of sweat on his forehead betrayed to me how great an effort he was making. "Your Messiah is impressive, Your Grace. But I think I would welcome the God emerging from the chrysalis of human failure more gratefully than your king who will come to impose his will upon us all."

He managed a thin smile. "An interesting little day-dream, Mr Tennel, if not a very original one. However...."

"But is it a day-dream, Your Grace? Or has it, perhaps, become a reality since yesterday morning?"

He made an impatient gesture.

"I know," I said. "But the evidence we have heard of the resurrection of Davidson has made a strong impression on us."

He sighed. "I won't ask for the name of your informant, but I would hazard a guess that she is a woman. Indeed, I would go so far as to say one particular woman. Am I right?"

"As a matter of fact, yes, you are."

He nodded. "I thought so. Davidson had a peculiar effect on women—at least, on women like Mary Magdala."

"I didn't say it was Mary Magdala."

"No. But I know it was she. You cannot control a nation like ours without reliable sources of information, Mr Tennel. Yes, he affected women of her type very profoundly, in an unhealthy fashion. When he was arrested, as perhaps you know, his men deserted him. Took to their heels and ran like the despicable rabble they are. At his execution not one of them was present, but there were several. . . ."

I said quickly, "John Zebedee. He was there, surely?"

He frowned. "He alone. And he will bear watching, Mr Tennel. He will bear watching."

"Isn't he, in fact, a cousin of yours, Your Grace?"

"Quite true, if a little beside the point." He gave me his mirthless smile. "It is a rare family that has no skeleton in its cupboard."

"I'm sorry, I interrupted you I'm afraid. You were saying about the women. . . ?"

"Ah yes, the women. They were all there, you know. At the execution. Most distressing and unnatural."

"Distressing, certainly."

"And unnatural," he said firmly. "What sort of a religious movement is it that can find so prominent a place within its organization for women?"

Spoken like a true Jew, I thought, remembering how, in the synagogue, the women were segregated, allowed in on sufferance as observers rather than as participators.

I said, "Some of the Greek cults. . .

"Exactly. The Greek cults. And we all know what they are like, do we not? Licensed immorality is perhaps the most charitable description of their rituals."

"They're said to be very poetic, Your Grace," I said mildly.

"A word currently synonymous with depravity. They are abominable, Mr Tennel. Primitive fertility rites dressed-up with sophisticated music and masquerading as religion. Disgusting."

I smiled to myself. He did the outraged conscience of Jewry extremely well.

"But even they," he said, "would scarcely countenance the presence of one so shameless as Mary Magdala. A sensual, brazen creature of the most unsavoury reputation."

"I must say, Your Grace, she didn't strike us as being at all like that. We found her quite charming."

He drew himself up in his chair. "Mr Tennel, there is no profit in discussing such a woman. Her notoriety speaks for itself."

But I was determined not to be bullied. "How well do you know her, Your Grace? Have you, for instance, ever met her personally?"

"No. Nor have I the slightest wish to do so. The reports of her character and activities are more than sufficient to. . . ."

I nodded. "Jesus Davidson, on the other hand, knew her very well indeed. And knowing her, gave her a place among his closest friends. An important and honourable place."

"Honourable, Mr Tennel? Hardly the correct word, I think. Her presence among those men was surely anything but honourable."

He was sitting very straight and tall now, the judge on the bench with all the moral authority of the law behind him. I thought, this is how he must have seen you when you pronounced sentence of death on him in the early hours of Friday morning.

I said, "I can't agree with you, Your Grace. Having listened to her account of. . ."

"Oh, please." He tilted his head in affront. "Let us not be naïve about this. When twelve men of no consequence —some of them married—leave their homes and take to the road; and when they are joined in their wanderings by a notoriously immoral woman—when that happens, Mr

Tennel, the conclusions one draws are surely obvious—and very much divorced from honour."

I watched the spittle drying on his thin lips and knew that in a twisted sort of way he was enjoying himself. There was a disquieting fascination in his ability to switch from the ecstatic chanting of the Messianic vision to this vindictive attack on a woman he had never met. I was reminded of the psychopath who, having committed a particularly brutal murder, returns to his room and spends an hour talking baby-talk to his budgerigar.

"I'm sorry, Mr Tennel," he said with well-assumed sadness, "but I did warn you, did I not, that there could be no profit in discussing her? Indeed, the more deeply one is compelled to probe into the affairs of Davidson, the more distasteful they become."

I said levelly, "It's not the lack of profit that disturbs me, Your Grace. It's the lack of charity."

Coldly angry, his eyes met mine. "Come, Mr Tennel, I cannot allow you to instruct me in the technicalities of my chosen profession. I see you are a kind-hearted man. It does you credit. Charity is one of God's gifts to us, and a valuable one. But it cannot be used as a cloak to cover evil. Charity, Mr Tennel, is not condoning what is wrong. It is, rather, that quality of the mind which enables us to condemn evil without hating the evil-doer. It is not uncharitable to describe Mary Magdala as an immoral woman, for that is what she is."

"I can only repeat," I said stolidly, "that our impression of her is quite different. We found her to be both modest and sincere. And I, for one, am disposed to take very seriously indeed her claim to have seen and talked to Davidson outside the tomb yesterday morning."

He sighed. "You are at liberty to do that, of course. But I must confess, Mr Tennel, that I find it disappointing that a man of your intelligence and experience should choose to accept the word of a—a belly-dancer turned camp-follower—" he gave the words a tremendous lip-licking emphasis—"in preference to the considered, and I may say expert, judgement of Lord Pilate and my-self." He spread his hands in a gesture of appeal, man-to-man and let's-be-sensible-about-this-shall-we? "The political and religious implications of what she claims to have seen are quite incalculable, Mr Tennel. The Governor-General and I understand that. And so, I am sure, do you. But does she understand it, Mr Tennel? Indeed, can she? A woman without education, living a life of vicious. . . ."

I cut him short, "She doesn't claim to understand it, Your Grace. Only to believe it. And, with the greatest respect, if in fact there has been a resurrection, I doubt if either you or Lord Pilate can find a category, political or religious, into which such an event can be fitted."

He nodded gravely. "What you are saying, Mr Tennel —and you are perfectly right—is that it is an impos-sibility."

"That," I said, "or a miracle."

He compressed his lips angrily, his eyebrows raised. We held him like that, in close-up, for a couple of seconds and then, just before he spoke, cut back to the studio. The effect that I hoped would stay in the viewers' minds was of a man disturbed by something wholly unexpected, brought up short at the end of a careful piece of rationalization by the startling discovery of a new element in the case—the one thing that, as a priest, he should have reckoned with from the beginning. The one thing he had failed to take into account.

I I

We were back in Kapper's office just after four. The girl brought in some coffee and I drank the first cup in one gulp. It was hot and sweet, and I needed it badly. I have a fairly low tolerance for dishonest churchmen and the interview with Caiaphas had left me tired and strained. I poured myself another cup and tried to relax.

"How was he?" Kapper said.

"Caiaphas?" I shrugged irritably. "Difficult."

"Ice and vinegar," Greg said, "with just a touch of bitters."

"Yes. Like that. If we'd had him plugged into a lie-detector he'd've blown every fuse in the Palace in the first five minutes."

Kapper nodded. "Did you manage to break him down at all?"

"Not so's you'd notice. But with a bit of careful editing it can be made to look as though we did."

"Is he worried, d'you think? About Davidson, I mean."

"I think he's trying not to be. He's worked over this grave-robbers-and-vandals theory, wrapped it up in a lot of theological double-talk and sold it to Pilate without even trying."

"Knowing Pilate, that wouldn't be difficult."

"Quite. All he's got to do now is persuade the peasants

to swallow it." I lit a cigarette. "I'll tell you one thing, Nick. He's really got his knife into the Magdala."

"Naturally," Kapper said. "He's a highly moral man."

"He's a twenty-two-carat bastard," Greg said savagely.

"That too. They usually go together." He sat back in his chair and put his hands behind his head. "Well, what d'you think now, Cass? Got enough to make it stick?"

"I don't know. I doubt it. But I don't see what more we can do." I looked at the sweep second hand jerking round the dial of the clock above his desk. It was always the same in this business. You never had enough time to do the job properly. Another twenty-four hours might see the whole thing settled one way or the other. But I was due on camera in less than five hours. The only consolation was that I could get my piece in before Caiaphas's official statement appeared in the papers the next morning.

"The trouble is, Nick," I said then, "we've got nobody respectable on Davidson's side."

Kapper sipped his coffee. "Does that worry you, Cass?"

"Not me. The viewers. It's going to throw them. If the Magdala was happily married, with three kids and a husband working in the bank, we might have a sporting chance. As it is, however much they want to believe her, they're still going to have doubts."

"Because of her background?"

I nodded. "You know what they're like. They kid themselves they're progressive and open-minded, but underneath they're as reactionary as all get out. They'll listen to every word she says, but they won't for one moment forget that she's an ex-belly-dancer."

"And Caiaphas? What'll they make of him, d'you think?"

"They'll hate his guts," I said wearily, "and believe him implicitly, right down the line. The public mind has a

147

built-in computer which insists, whatever sort of programme you feed into it, that priests always tell the truth.
If Caiaphas says the Magdala's a naughty girl and Davidson's a dead heretic, then that's what they'll believe."

"They could do worse," Kapper said. "I don't like
him any more than you do, Cass, but you must admit it's
a perfectly rational view."

"Oh, it's rational," I said. "That's what's the matter
with it. It's too damned rational."

Kapper pursed his lips. "If they accept it, it'll save an
awful lot of grief."

"Look," I said angrily, "he's lying. All that stuff about
the guards being drunk and the body being snatched—it's
all lies, Nick. Whatever happened at that tomb yesterday
morning, one thing's for sure—there wasn't a grave-
robber within a hundred miles of it."

"Perhaps not. But it's a nice tidy answer. No loose-ends.
No hocus-pocus. It may not be strictly accurate, but at
least it makes sense."

"Meaning a resurrection doesn't?"

He shrugged. "Well, does it?"

I rubbed my hand over my face, feeling the skin dry and
tight, the tiredness burning behind my eyelids. "You still
think I'm wrong?"

"I don't know, Cass. I just don't know. You've gone
overboard on this resurrection theory. It's no longer a
piece of straight reporting to you. It's a case you've got to
win."

Put like that I didn't like it, but I couldn't deny it. I'd
begun by wanting fair play for Davidson; a chance to tell
his side of the story. I was angered by Pilate's bland
cynicism and sickened by the way Davidson had been
bundled off to the gallows—given a bad name and hanged.
At that stage all I'd wanted to do was to find something

good to say about him; some motive greater than a greed for political power. Talking to Regem Zaccheus and the Magdala I had found that motive—that idealistic conception of a new society, coupled with a quite extraordinary concern for the common people. And listening to them talking about it, and seeing it somehow alive and real in their personalities, I had begun to want it to be true.

Somewhere along the line I had found myself forced to make a choice, not just between Pilate and Zaccheus, or Caiaphas and the Magdala, but between the two worlds they represented. Between the world I knew and lived in— the gimcrack political structure of lies and treachery and power backed by violence—and the world Davidson had promised to his followers. I told myself now, struggling with the tension and fatigue in my mind, that if I believed Davidson was alive again it was only because I believed in the reality of his world—the world I had glimpsed in the reckless, cheerful confidence of Regem Zaccheus, the deeply-moving sincerity of Mary Magdala.

Kapper was watching me intently. "If you looked at it objectively," he said, "you'd be the first to admit you've got nothing like enough evidence."

How much evidence is enough? I thought. This is something you either believe or you don't.

"The trouble is," Kapper said, "you've let yourself get involved. I warned you about that. You should be standing above and behind it, Cass. Weighing it up, making a disinterested assessment. But you're not doing that. Not any more. You're inside it, sweating it out, trying to make it come out the way you think it should. And all because of a girl with red hair and the ability to tell her story extremely well."

I said quickly, "It's not just her, Nick. There're the others. Zaccheus shutting-up shop. Sanballet doing his

149

tight-lipped, honour-of-the-regiment act. Nicodemus and Pilate dithering about. Thomas Didymus breaking his heart. And now that cold devil Caiaphas lying his way out of a tight corner. It all adds up to something. You can't get away from that."

"I'm not trying to get away from anything, Cass. All I'm saying is that you can't go on camera tonight and state categorically that there has been a resurrection. Not on the basis of the evidence you've collected."

He was right, of course. The evidence was not conclusive. I was in the position of a lawyer who knows his client is innocent but hasn't quite enough evidence to convince the jury. In those circumstances all he can do is try. And I was determined to try. I had looked round the edge of the door and seen the new world Davidson had talked about. Whatever happened I was going to keep my foot in that door and stop it closing.

"I can't agree," I said.

Kapper sighed. "Damn it all, Cass, this is supposed to be factual reporting, not Armchair Mystery Theatre. All right, let's examine the facts. Pilate says there's been no resurrection. Nicodemus says there can't have been one. Caiaphas supports this view and supplies a rational explanation of the rumour free of charge. It may not be the right explanation, but at least it'll keep things ticking over quietly until the right one turns up."

Pilate, Nicodemus, Caiaphas, all pressing hard to slam the door shut. The Church and the State terrified by the vision of freedom they had seen. Who was I to hold the door open against them? Who, for that matter, was Davidson to open the door in the first place?

I got up and walked across to the window and looked out over the city. Was Davidson alive, as Mary Magdala believed? And if he was, where was he now? Somewhere in that ancient labyrinth of streets, holed-up in a room in the house of a friend? Or out beyond the Mount of Olives, travelling the country road to Nazareth and the north? What did he look like after three days of death? And what were the plans in his head as he went to brief his little band of followers up there by the blue waters of Galilee?

These were the questions we should have to face, the questions the viewers would ask. What sort of answers would we give them when the phones started ringing and the letters came flooding in? And would any of them sound even half as convincing as the neat little explanation Caiaphas had presented?

Below me, at the Jaffa Gate, there were long queues for the country buses going out to Bethlehem and Kerioth and Beer-Sheba, the people standing patiently in the late afternoon sunshine with their bags and shopping-baskets. Husbands going home from work, mothers with their children, farmers going back for the milking after a day in the market. There were people like these standing in queues in every city in the world. How would they react tonight when they sat in front of their little screens and were baldly informed that God was hanged in Jerusalem last Friday afternoon and was now walking about alive again somewhere near Tiberias?

There was an army half-track parked in the shadow of the gate tower, its twin machine-guns cocked idly at the sky. The crew lounged in the shade, tough and capable in their khaki-drill and black berets, the blancoed webbing dusty white against their drab shirts. I watched them laughing and smoking, confident in their youthful arrogance against the drooping patience of the queues. I thought of the immense political and military power they represented and wondered what sort of an army God, as a young man risen from the dead, could set against the legions of Rome. I remembered Zaccheus throwing back his head to laugh in the quiet street, and Thomas Didymus hunched in his chair under the studio lights, and the bright, vulnerable innocence of Mary Magdala. "We have an ancient dream of freedom," Nicodemus had said. Could men and women like these triumph where Rome had failed and build a kingdom based not upon tanks and missiles and the fear of marching men but upon love and liberty and the quiet virtues of peace? If men like Pilate and Caiaphas could have God killed, could God, rising to live again, give life to these and all men—bring us out of the trap we had ourselves created and set us free at last?

The soldiers were stamping on their cigarette-ends and climbing into the half-track. The guns swung down and the engine roared and the ugly vehicle crawled down the ramp on its metal tracks and rumbled away down the road, its shadow chopping through the queues like a blunted scythe. I watched it crunch round the corner in a blue haze of exhaust fumes and some words of a Jewish poem came half-remembered into my mind: "Lord, rescue my darling, my darling from the lions."

"It isn't any good, is it, Cass?" Kapper had come to stand at my shoulder and his words in my ear were like a voice in my own mind.

"I still think the Magdala saw him," I said stubbornly.

"Then you go on thinking that, Cass," Kapper said gently. "But let's play it safe tonight, shall we? No need to draw conclusions. Let 'em hear both sides and make up their own minds."

It was good advice; sound, safe, and strictly according to the book. It was, moreover, a line I had taken on many previous occasions—disinterested, objective, uninvolved; the line I had determined originally to take with this story. I watched the light change and mellow across the roofs of the city and wondered wearily why I was so reluctant to take it now.

When I turned and looked at him, Kapper was half-smiling. In his narrow, intelligent face his eyes pleaded with me to be sensible.

"What d'you think, Nick?" I said, making one last try. "Not as a producer, as a man. What d'you really think?"

His smile faded momentarily and I saw a small flicker of doubt in his eyes—or was it perhaps only irritation?—and then he grinned and clapped his hand on my shoulder. "I think you should get your head down for a couple of hours, Cass. You've got a good programme there. You don't want to spoil it by being too tired to put it across. Can't have the customers complaining that you go on camera looking like death warmed-up, can we?"

I think it was the only time I heard Nick Kapper speak out of character. The good-humour in his voice was as false as a gold tooth.

I said, "All right, Nick. But you might have chosen a happier simile. In the circumstances."

12

Kapper came through on the studio phone during the Caiaphas piece with the news that Patros had agreed to let us have extra time.

"How much?" I said.

"Four minutes."

"That's no good."

"I know, Cass, but it's the best I could do. I had to weep blood to get that much."

"Thanks, Nick," I said, and meant it. Getting four extra minutes out of Patros was a considerable achievement. "What've they got on the Rome channel after us?"

"Spanish flamenco music. Twenty-five minutes."

"Pre-recorded or live?"

"Pre-recorded. And a repeat at that."

Which was quite extraordinary luck. If it had been something about politics or sport Patros would have shut down on us without hesitation. But a programme of music was something else again. Patros was tone-deaf and indifferent to music. The chances were that if we ran on over the four minutes he would let it go. He'd hit the ceiling of course, afterwards. But he wouldn't stop the programme.

"Right," I said. "We'll press on and risk it. Didymus after this. Then Cleopas to finish. Okay?"

"Didymus on top of Caiaphas is going to take some answering, Cass."

"I know. But if this Cleopas character is anything like you say he is he'll give us our answer. An eye-witness and respectable. It's exactly what we need."

"Well, I dunno." He sounded doubtful.

We had thrashed out the final pattern before and during the camera rehearsal earlier that evening. As usual it had been like working in a partially-demolished mental hospital with a clutch of highly-intelligent specialists all suffering from acute paranoia. Men wearing headphones shouted to invisible assistants. Lighting technicians—a notoriously phlegmatic breed—argued doggedly with camera-crews—second only to fighter pilots in their reliance upon hand gestures to illustrate their words. Assistant secretaries picked their way anxiously across the floor over tangled heaps of high-voltage cables. At the heart of this chaos, right in the centre of the studio under the full glare of the lights, two engineers in white coats poked long-handled screwdrivers irritably into the exposed interior of the number one camera, looking, as Kapper testily said, like a couple of petrol-pump attendants pretending to be doctors.

Upstairs in the production-box things were quieter but no less bizarre. Above the main console the multiple monitor-screens flickered in the half-light, presenting a series of unrelated pictures in feverish succession, jerking them on and off like a group of automated salesmen desperately bringing out sample after sample in the hope of making a sale. Girls with stop-watches muttered interminable count-downs to themselves as they checked the tele-cine reels cue-chart. At irregular and disconcerting intervals someone snapped on the speakers and the soaring cacophony of the studio leaped into the room like a tiger from its cage.

But Kapper and I were used to this. It had long ago ceased to bewilder us. Indeed we found it both normal and stimulating. We settled down comfortably with the rough script, lit cigarettes and got to work.

"Pilate first, I think," Kapper said. "May as well begin with our feet on the ground, whatever weird flights of fancy we indulge in later. Then the army bod—what's his name again. . . ?"

Miriam, his secretary said, "Major Sanballet."

"Yes. Him. Then—let's see—Nicodemus?" He raised his eyebrows and looked at me.

"Nicodemus next, by all means," I said equably.

He nodded. "Then Zaccheus—to open for your side, so to speak. And after him, for what he's worth, friend Didymus."

I said, "Who, on the surface at least, is on your side."

"On the side of common-sense, anyway," he said mildly. He checked his list. "That leaves the Magdala and Caiaphas. I would think in that order."

I shook my head. "Caiaphas first. I want the Magdala to have the last word."

"Sorry, Cass. I can't accept that. Much as I dislike him, Caiaphas is the High Priest."

"What's that got to do with it?"

He sighed patiently. "Whatever we think of the man, we're bound, in common courtesy, to respect his office. With Pilate opening for the State it's S.O.P. to let Caiaphas close for the Church."

"Oh for God's sake, Nick," I said. "This is no time to quibble about protocol. My job is to put this story across with as much force as possible, and. . . ."

"And my job is to do what little I can to prevent you from making a complete fool of yourself."

The noise from the studio blared over our heads for a moment and we sat and glared at each other. The effects of the couple of hours' sleep I'd had were beginning to wear off. I could feel the tiredness seeping back into my body like a fever temperature rising to overcome the temporary relief of four aspirin. Only the fact that Miriam was there prevented me from losing my temper.

I said stiffly, "That may be your view. It's most certainly not mine."

"Look, Cass," he said, and I could hear the anger cracking the surface of his voice, "it's not only a question of protocol. It's a question of making the most of what you've got. If you put Caiaphas on first, immediately after Didymus, you may as well forget the Magdala altogether for all the effect she'll have." He waited for me to say something but I only shook my head. "It's like you said yourself. She's not respectable. You've got to let her say her piece before Caiaphas starts smacking his lips over her. It's your only hope."

"You're joking," I said. "You know damn well if he comes on last—in the key position—he'll steam-roller her into the ground."

"I'm sorry. That's a chance you'll have to take."

We argued about it some more but in the end, under protest and against my better judgement, I had agreed.

I said now, "It's a good pattern, Nick. The Magdala to back up Zaccheus. Then Caiaphas here explaining it all smoothly away, putting everthing nearly in its place. Then Didymus, tolling like a funeral bell, disturbing them all over again. And finally, Cleopas, respectable as a rolled umbrella, to jerk their minds into focus and clinch it for us."

I screwed up my eyes, looking past the banks of lights to the faint blue glow coming from the sound-proofed window of the production box, visualizing him there at the other end of the telephone-line, willing me to be sensible.

"You're taking an unnecessarily big chance, in my opinion," he said tartly. "This Cleopas chap's a decent enough little man. But he's an unknown quantity. If he doesn't measure up, or if Patros decides to be bloody-minded and cut us off, you'll be up the creek. I hope you realize that."

"Yes, Nick," I said. "I do."

I heard him sigh. "Okay."

"Thanks."

"Not at all." His voice was wearily polite. "Just don't expect me to be enthusiastic about it, that's all. I've known you too long to relish the prospect of watching you commit professional suicide."

"I doubt if it will come to anything quite so dramatic as that," I said. But he had already hung up.

The floor-manager signed to me that the interview with Caiaphas was coming to its close. I sat forward in my chair, leaning my arms comfortably on the desk, and watched the face of the High Priest fill the monitor screen. I was delighted to see that his expression of irritated distaste in the final couple of seconds could, as I had hoped, be interpreted equally well as being one of astonished uneasiness.

I took my cue and raised my eyebrows at Number One camera.

"A miracle? Is this perhaps the answer to the riddle? His Grace the High Priest has given us a careful and indeed an extremely credible account of the events leading up to yesterday morning's occurrence. This is no less than we had expected from him with his experience and special knowledge. We can all be grateful that the complex and sometimes controversial affairs of the Church in this troubled province of the Empire are so firmly in the control of an administrator as capable as Lord Caiaphas." It is one of the oldest tricks in the business, but still surprisingly effective. They do it with pyramids of tin cans at country fairs. You build them up to knock them down. And the better you build the more satisfying the fall. "But it is clear that a miracle is something with which he has not reckoned as yet. Can it be that his sense of responsibility for the spiritual welfare of the nation, involving him as it must do in the day-to-day handling of practical issues concerning the keeping of the peace and the security of the people—can it be that these immediate issues, focused with exceptional sharpness during a religious festival, have caused him to overlook the possibility of a miracle?

"In the minds of the ordinary people of this land miracles and Jesus Davidson go together. There is, of course, a difference between the healing of a leper and an act of self-resurrection. But it is a difference of degree only. And Davidson himself spoke on a number of occasions of his resurrection.

"We have been fortunate to obtain an interview with one of those who were closest to him throughout his public career; a man who heard him say, quite categorically, that he would come back after death. His name is Thomas Didymus. . . .". .

Didymus appeared on the monitor, hunched and miserable, the lank hair falling across his forehead. Through the speaker his flat voice made that devastating opening statement: "I've nothing to hide, mister. He's dead, and that's all there is to it."

The phone beside me rang briefly. I picked up the receiver.

"Inspiring, isn't he?" Kapper said. "I hope you know what you're doing, Cass. Every word this boy speaks is another nail in your coffin."

"Let me worry about that. What've you done with Cleopas?"

"I've got him here."

"Right. Send him down now, will you? I shall want a forty second lead-in after Didymus and then we'll take him on live."

"For better, for worse," Kapper said. "Till Patros doth you part." Which meant that he was over the hump and committed, and, in his own cautious way, beginning to enjoy himself. I put the phone down and got up and walked over to the studio door. Kapper's secretary came in with Cleopas, made the introductions, and left us.

I took him across to the set and settled him in a second chair placed at the left-hand end of the desk and angled to face me. I sat down in my own chair and had a good look at him.

He was, to my relief, a complete contrast to Didymus; a slight, neat little man wearing a dark-grey lounge suit, a white shirt and a plain blue tie. There was a white handkerchief tucked into the breast pocket of his jacket and his shoes were polished and a little rounder at the toe than was fashionable. He looked to be in his late thirties, his hair going thin at the temples and brushed back from his rather small face. The general impression was of an accountant; a junior partner perhaps in a slightly old-fashioned but thoroughly reputable firm. I smiled at him approvingly. When I put him on camera the viewers would see a man they could trust, decent, respectable, pleasant.

Like most people who find themselves for the first

time under the brash lights of a television studio he was a little apprehensive. He sat on the edge of his chair and kept darting sidelong glances at the cameras. I would have preferred to spend a few minutes in small talk to relax him, but the interview with Didymus was more than half over and there was no time. I just had to hope that what Kapper had said about him was true, and that once I got him started on his story he would forget to be nervous.

One of the make-up girls brought her towel and cosmetic box and began to powder his forehead. He looked at me, embarrassed.

"She's just taking the shine off, Mr Cleopas," I said, smiling. "She does it to all the boys."

"What d'you want me to do?" he said.

"Just relax and talk to me. Don't worry about the cameras or any of these technical people. Just imagine we're sitting at a table together, somewhere quiet, having a drink and discussing the news of the day. Okay?"

He nodded and managed a smile as the girl finished his face. He watched her walk away into the shadows behind the cameras with something of the expression of a small boy left at the dentist's by his mother for the first time. I glanced at the monitor.

"The producer was telling me that you've actually seen Jesus Davidson since yesterday morning. Is that right?"

His face suddenly came alive. "It is indeed. My brother-in-law and I—we were on the bus, you see. Yesterday afternoon—well, early evening really. And this man got on just outside the. . . ."

I felt the relief wash over me. "Good," I said. "Don't tell me now. Wait till we're on camera."

Which really was doing it the hard way, but I had taken an immediate liking to this gentle, quiet-spoken man, and so much depended on his story coming through fresh and

unrehearsed. In any event, we were now so far out on a
limb with Patros that an inch or two more would make no
difference.

"How will I know?" he said. "When to begin, I mean?"

"Just leave it to me."

The floor-manager said loudly, "Thirty seconds."

"Sit back and relax," I said to Cleopas. "You haven't
a thing to worry about." And added under my breath,
"Unlike some of us here tonight."

"Quiet please," the floor-manager said, and a moment
later pointed his finger at me.

In the back of my mind, during the last twenty minutes
or so, I had been turning over possible ways of bringing
Simon Cleopas into the programme. We had not time
for elaborate introductions, which was perhaps just
as well since I knew so little about him. Nor was there
anything I could say which would soften the tragic
impact of the interview with Didymus and lead naturally
and smoothly into what I hoped was going to be a
quite different point of view. In the end I decided to
offer no comment on Didymus and let Cleopas come
as a completely unknown quantity, presented to the
viewers with the briefest of explanations.

I looked into the lens of the camera. "Up until half an
hour ago the story was as inconclusive as that. But since
we came on the air there had been a new development.
Additional evidence is now available." I should, strictly,
have said additional information. But I deliberately
chose the word evidence with its implications of a court
of law and a trial. I wanted the viewers to be gripped
by the drama of the situation, and to feel, as I did,
personally involved in it. "Here to tell us about it is
Mr Simon Cleopas who comes from the village of Emmaus, about seven miles out of the city."

13

I saw his face come up on the monitor-screen, small,
ordinary, wearing a slightly strained expression. I had a
moment of cold panic. How could I have persuaded myself to put so insignificant a nonentity into the key position
on the programme? A man I knew nothing about, except
that he claimed to have seen Davidson alive after death.
I watched him turning his head uneasily, trying to avoid
the unblinking stare of the camera. I knew it was shyness
and nerves, but the effect on the viewers would be one of
furtiveness. After the Magdala's radiant poise and the
rock-steady authority of Caiaphas it was little short of
disastrous. I had to pump some confidence into him
quickly, or else get him off the screen.

I knew that if I began by asking him questions about
his background it would only increase his self-conscious-
ness. All I could do was to push him without ceremony
into the deep end of his story, and hope it was a good one
and that he would swim. I turned to face him. "Mr
Cleopas, is it true that you've seen Jesus Davidson alive
and well in the last twenty-four hours?"

And immediately my panic vanished and I knew that the
gamble was going to pay off. It was like being face to face
with a panel of twenty or more switches and by some lucky

chance pressing the right one. The strain went out of his face, he looked squarely into the camera-lens, his voice was clear, without a trace of nervousness. "Yes," he said. "Quite true."

"When did you see him?"

"Yesterday afternoon. And again last night."

I waited as long as I dared, letting his words hang in the air. And then I said, "Would you like to tell us about it?"

"Yes, of course." He leaned forward, eager, relaxed. "We were on the four o'clock bus to Emmaus, my brother-in-law and I. We'd been in town for the Festival, you see. We'd planned to go back home yesterday morning, but we hung on in case there was any more news."

He was just as Kapper had described him on the phone, excited, transparently honest, bursting to tell his story. Coming immediately after the sombre agony of Thomas Didymus he was exactly the sort of person with whom the viewers could identify themselves—a gentle, matter-of-fact man involved in something oddly mysterious, but managing nevertheless to keep both his feet firmly on the ground. Looking at him you felt that it was entirely appropriate—indeed almost inevitable—that he should have met God on a bus.

"News about the resurrection, you mean?" I said.

He nodded. "That's right. We'd heard the rumour, of course. And naturally we were upset and confused. I was all for staying over until today, but my sister's a bit of a worrier and my brother-in-law thought it best that we should go home and perhaps come back in again this morning."

This was really translating it down to the viewers' level. Two anonymous citizens scratching their honest heads over bus time-tables and a nervous wife. Nothing could be more normal and, as I hoped, convincing.

"The bus was three parts empty," he said, "and we settled ourselves on the back seat and began to go over the events of the week-end again for about the ninety-ninth time. Trying to make some sort of sense out of it all, but not getting very far, I'm afraid." He smiled apologetically. "And then, about a mile out of the city, this man got on and came right down to the back and joined us."

"Davidson?"

"Well, that's the funny thing. You see, we didn't recognize him. We'd been followers of his for nearly two years. Not important ones, don't run away with that idea. We're not in the same class as Peter Johnson or Matthew Levison. But we believed in him. We'd heard him speak dozens of times—never missed the chance whenever he was anywhere near Jerusalem. And we'd both talked to him personally on a number of occasions. But when he got on that bus yesterday afternoon he was a complete stranger to us." He shook his head impatiently, like a man bewildered by his own stupidity. "And there was something else odd about it too. He didn't seem to have any idea at all about what had been going on over the week-end in the city. He joined in our conversation, but we had to tell him about the execution last Friday and the rumours of yesterday's resurrection. From the questions he asked he hadn't heard about any of it."

"When you told him, what did he say?"

"Oh my word, Mr Tennel, what didn't he say? He started right back there in the time of Moses and worked up through the prophets—Isaiah and Amos—all the classic quotations—right up to the present day. Had it all at his finger-tips. Marvellous. We just sat and gaped at him. I mean, in a way it was old stuff to us. Every Jew has it pumped into him from the day he starts school—the story of the Messiah. But this man. . . ."

"Just a moment," I said. "When you say the Messiah do you, in fact, mean God?"

"You could say that, yes. Some of our priests—the scholars, you know—they'd probably want to argue about that. They usually describe him as the Son of God. But so far as I can see it amounts to the same thing. And, as I say, we've all been brought up on the Messiah story. Heard it hundreds of times. But not the way this man put it over. All those bits and pieces of prophecy—the difficult passages the priests spend half their lives discussing—he just fitted them together like—well, like assembling one of those do-it-yourself kits. Made the whole thing suddenly clear and sort of—well, inevitable. Especially the resurrection."

I looked at him gratefully, and with a certain misgiving. It was at this precise point that Nicodemus had stopped short, defeated in his thinking by the fact of death. I hardly dared to hope that someone as unremarkable as Simon Cleopas could break through where a scholar of the Sanhedrin had failed. But if he could, if he had found, or been given, the answer. . . .

I said slowly, "I'd like to be quite clear about this, Mr Cleopas. Are you saying that a resurrection is an integral part of the Messiah story?"

"It's the climax of it. The final miraculous piece that makes sense of all the rest." He moved his hands in a gesture of rounded completion. "The Messiah comes, but nobody recognizes him. Nobody wants him. He isn't in the least like we'd expected him to be. Instead of crowning him king, we execute him. We don't know who he is, so we get rid of him. Or try to. But Messiah is the conqueror of death. And on the third day he comes back to establish his kingdom."

"Messiah is the conqueror of death". They were the exact words that Nicodemus had used. But for him they had been final proof that Davidson was not—could not have been—the Messiah. "Messiah cannot die"—that was what he had said. And if there was no death in the Messiah story, how could there be a resurrection?

I said, "But if the Messiah is the conqueror of death, how can he die?"

"Unless he meets death face to face," Simon Cleopas said, "how can he conquer it?"

I remembered the anxiety of Nicodemus, the flicker of fear in the cold eyes of the High Priest. Was this the question they were afraid to answer? The incisive, demanding question that mocked their theological sophistry?

"That's what he made clear to us, on the bus," he said then. "If the Messiah is to rescue men he must share in the fact of death. He must die, as all men must die. We cannot share in the life of his kingdom unless he shares in our death."

"But surely," I said, as much for the viewers as for myself, "he need not have died? If he was the Messiah, surely he could have used his power to avoid death at the end?"

He shook his head. "No. That's what they said—his enemies in the Sanhedrin. 'If you are the Son of God, save yourself.'"

"Seems a reasonable sort of idea to me."

"Oh, he could've done that. No trouble at all. But it wouldn't have helped us, would it? I mean, when it came our turn to die, the fact that he had arranged a last-minute rescue for himself last Friday afternoon wouldn't

167

have made any difference to us then. You don't conquer death by avoiding it, Mr Tennel. You conquer it by accepting it and breaking through to life on the other side. Because he has done that we don't need to be afraid of death any more."

He spoke the words with simple dignity, as relaxed and at home in front of the camera now as a news-reader. I had the odd feeling that our roles had been reversed; that he was somehow interviewing me. I shot a quick glance at the clock and said, "And while he was explaining all this, you still didn't recognize him?"

He nodded. "Not until we got to Emmaus. He said he was going on up to Nazareth but my brother-in-law persuaded him to come home with us. 'It'll only be pot-luck,' he said, 'but you're very welcome to share it.' So he went with us to the house. And that's where it happened."

"What exactly did happen there, Mr Cleopas?"

"We recognized him. At supper. We were sitting round the table ready to begin. My brother-in-law invited him, as the guest, to say grace. It's a custom we have among ourselves, you know. Well, he picked up the loaf, gave thanks, and broke it. And in that moment we looked at him and knew who he was."

"Jesus Davidson?"

"Yes, of course. Jesus the Messiah. He was dead and is alive again. Blessed is he."

There was no mistaking his conviction. His voice rose a shade, a sort of congregational response to the professional priestly chant Nicodemus had used in quoting from the prophets. His eyes were bright and there was a kind of solemn happiness in his expression.

"You're quite sure of that?"

"Positive."

"A trick of the light, perhaps? A certain familiar intonation in the voice? A psychological reflex coming at the end of a long confusing day?" I threw the suggestions at him in rapid succession. It was like trying to dam a river by throwing in match-sticks. He swept them aside with a gesture.

"You can call it what you like," he said. "Long words don't worry me. I know who he was. We sat there next to him, as close as I am to you now, and watched him break that bread. And it was Jesus. No two ways about that. It was Jesus."

I nodded. "And then what happened?"

"He disappeared." He said it bluntly, without a tremor. "Vanished. One moment he was there, offering us the bread. The next, he was gone." He laughed excitedly. "Talk about panic-stations. We rushed out of the house, hired a car at the local garage, and fairly tore back here. Left the supper on the table and my sister in a flap and just took off." He blew out his cheeks, his face shining under the lights. "What a ride that was. We just made it through the gate before the curfew, got to the house, paid the driver off, and went up the stairs two at a time to tell the others."

"And what did they say?"

"Oh it was a proper bombshell, I can tell you. They were all there in the house, eating supper. We burst in like a hurricane and told them we'd seen him." He spread his hands and rounded his eyes, acting out the astonishment. "You should've seen their faces, Marvellous."

"They believed you, did they?"

"Well, more or less. Some did. Some weren't so sure. Still, it didn't matter, because while we were still in the middle of telling them, he came in."

"You mean, Davidson himself?"

"Yes. The door was locked, but in he came. Straight through the wall."

"Like a ghost, you mean?"

"Ghost? Oh no. That's what they thought. I've never seen such a collection of frightened faces. Some of the women screamed."

"That's understandable."

"Yes, of course. He understood too. He held out his hands and told us to touch him. 'Ghosts don't have flesh and blood and bones,' he said. 'Touch me. Make sure it's really me.'"

"Did that convince them?"

"Pretty well. Except that, even then, we wondered a bit. I mean, it seemed too good to be true. But he saw our difficulty. He looked at the remains of the supper on the table. 'Give me a little of that fish,' he said. Somebody gave him a plate and a fork and he just stood there and ate the fish, slowly, as though he was enjoying it."

"I see." I managed, with an effort, to say it calmly. Inside me the tension was coiled tightly as I caught the infection of his excitement. I told myself even Patros couldn't brush this aside.

"Don't talk to me about ghosts," he said, with splendid contempt. "Ghosts don't stand around eating supper."

"That's true. On the other hand, people don't just appear and disappear through the wall, do they?"

But he was ready for that, as he had been ready for all my questions with that simple, devastating logic of his.

"Not ordinary people. Not people like you and me. But this is God, Mr Tennel. He's not tied down in time and place like us. He's free. Way out there on the other side of death, the king in the glory of his kingdom. You can't

170

expect him to be just ordinary."

"No."

"I mean, it stands to reason. He wouldn't be God if he was like us now, would he?"

"I suppose not."

"I've heard him speak, and seen him eat. I know it's him, Mr Tennel, I know it is. I know this too, from now on wherever men sit down to eat together he'll be there with them."

I looked at him with great affection. He had done more than I'd dared to hope. He had stepped into the key position in the programme and held it magnificently. All I had to do now was to get him off camera and finish the piece quickly, while the impact he had made was still fresh in the viewers' minds. The safest thing to do was simply to thank him and leave it at that. But I had gambled so hard on him and he had paid such handsome dividends that I decided to risk one more throw of the dice.

I said, "Mr Cleopas, the authorities are taking a very serious view of this. You've seen the patrols in the city. You know about the curfew. Aren't you just a little afraid of what might happen to you after telling this story to-night?"

He faced the camera, his face sober. "Well, yes, in a way I suppose I am. I mean, I've never been one for sticking my neck out before. Kept in the background, sort of thing. Only now, well, it doesn't matter any more. You see, the worst they can do is to kill me. And death isn't important now. He's made that clear enough. Death isn't the end, it's only the beginning.

"Up to yesterday morning we only had half a life. People like you and me—half alive, that's all we were. But now—now it's different. He's alive again. And because he's alive, we're alive too. Really alive, for the very first time.

"You know something, Mr Tennel?" he said, and his voice was quiet but strong, like a hand reaching out in confidence. "It's like being born again. That's what it is, being born again."

14

I nodded to him to sit still and turned to face Number One camera for the summing-up. I had to be quick now. According to the studio clock we were nearly seven minutes over time.

"So there it is," I said. "As complete a picture as we can give you of yesterday's astonishing events in this ancient capital city of the Jews. Has Jesus Davidson come back from the dead? Was he just a megalomaniac, a young religious fanatic dabbling in politics, or is he, in actual fact, God?"

Out of the corner of my eye I saw the studio door open briefly and Kapper's secretary come in.

"The official view, at the Residency and at the High Priest's Palace, is that this is simply a dangerous rumour put about by a group of disillusioned men who have stolen his body from the tomb in a last desperate attempt to vindicate their leader. . . ."

Miriam was whispering urgently to the floor-manager now. She held a sheet of paper in her hand and was pointing at me. A message from Patros? But Kapper would surely hold on to that now and at least let me wind-up the programme in peace.

". . . But an increasing number of ordinary men and women are rejoicing here tonight because they have seen him and spoken with him, and are convinced beyond threat or argument that he is alive. . . ."

I saw the floor-manager shrug his shoulders and take the paper from her. He walked quickly on to the side of the set and stood at the end of my desk, just out of the camera's range.

". . . For these people, who would seem to have no particular axe to grind, the rumour is no rumour at all. It is, in the most exact sense of the words, God's truth."

The floor-manager put the piece of paper flat on the desk and slid it towards me. I picked it up and glanced rapidly at the words typed in double-spacing on it, words that danced and blurred in front of my eyes for a moment, and then stood out suddenly in sharp focus as the impact of their message hit my mind.

I looked up at the camera. "Here is a news-flash that has just been handed to me. I'll read it:

"Two Jewish soldiers were arrested in a cabaret in the Old Quarter about half-an-hour ago. They are to be charged with drunkeness and disturbing the peace.

"They claim to be members of the guard detail on the tomb of Jesus Davidson. They both had a considerable amount of money in their pockets. They said that they received this money from the High Priest's secretary as a bribe to spread the rumour that the tomb was robbed while they were asleep on duty.

"In fact, they said, they were not asleep. There was a violent earthquake early yesterday morning; the tomb burst open; paralysed with terror they saw a figure dressed in dazzling white sitting at the open mouth of the tomb. They said—and here I quote the precise words—'His face was like lightning.'

"A full enquiry is to be held to discover how these men

174

escaped earlier this evening from the barracks where they were being held in close arrest.

"As he was being led out of the cabaret by the military police one of the soldiers said—and again I quote—'It doesn't matter what you do to me now. I've had it anyway. I've seen God's angel face to face, and that's death for any man.'"

I laid the sheet of paper down beside the bowl of flowers, wilting a little now after so long under the hot lights, and met the black glassy stare of the camera for the last time.

"One more piece in this curious puzzle of rumour and counter-rumour, of miracle and disturbing fact. For the soldier, what happened at the tomb of Jesus Davidson yesterday morning means death. For Miss Magdala, Mr Cleopas and their friends it means new life. Only time will show us who is right."

I leaned back slowly in my chair to cue Kapper and the floor-manager. The picture on the monitor mixed to the bowl of flowers, zoomed in until they filled the screen, and cut to a medium-shot of Patros in the Rome studio.

"Thank you, Cass Tennel." I looked at him carefully as his voice grated through the speaker, but he gave no indication of what he was thinking. Poker-faced, unemotional, he sat in the centre of the screen, the classic embodiment of impartiality. "That brings us to the end of this special report from Jerusalem. Good night."

The little screen went blank. The camera-men were unplugging their headphones and climbing down off the dollies. The big banks of overhead lights flicked off and the studio was suddenly, restfully gloomy. I stood up and stretched and rubbed my eyes. There was a dull nagging ache between my shoulders and I was desperately tired.

"Was that all right, Mr Tennel?"

I had forgotten Simon Cleopas. I turned and managed a smile. "It was exactly right, thank you very much indeed. Couldn't have been better if we'd rehearsed it all afternoon."

He nodded. "I was scared stiff when we started, but as soon as you asked me. . . ."

He broke off awkwardly as the phone on the desk rang. I picked up the receiver.

"Oh, Mr Tennel," it was Kapper's secretary, "Mr Kapper says could you please come up here straightaway. Mr Patros is on the wire from Rome and would like a word with you."

"Okay, Miriam. Thanks."

I put the phone down and said to Cleopas, "Look, my master in Rome wants to talk to me. Would you mind hanging on here for a couple of minutes? I won't be long, and then we can go and get a cup of coffee or something."

I walked across the studio to the door. One of the camera-men called out, "Nice going, Mr Tennel." I waved my hand and went out into the corridor and up the little staircase to the production box. Kapper was sitting on the edge of the console with the phone in his hand. Under the shaded lights his face was pale and tired.

"He's here now, Drewy," he said, and handed me the phone.

"Yes. Drewy?"

"Tennel?"

"Yes."

"You do surprise me. I imagined you'd still be waffling away in front of the camera."

I closed my eyes and said nothing. He was the boss. If he chose to spin it out slowly that was his privilege.

"Have you any idea at all—however vague—as to how

long you over-ran on tonight's little effort? Or are you now living in your own private little version of eternity, way out beyond the reach of clocks?"

"I'm sorry," I said. "I'm afraid we did run on a bit."

"Eight minutes fifty, to be precise."

"Oh-oh. That much? Sorry about that, Drewy."

"Don't apologize. It was a damned good story."

I blinked in surprise. "You mean you liked it?"

"Very much. I don't believe a word of it, of course. But it was good stuff, Cass, and you put it over well. One of your best."

Kapper passed me a cigarette and flicked his lighter. I took a long, deep pull at it and said, "You don't think he's alive, then?"

I heard him chuckle. "Do me a favour, Cass. I don't believe pigs can fly, either."

"Yes, but this is serious, Drewy. I mean, what about Mary Magdala and this Cleopas chap? Don't you think they're genuine in what they...?"

"The stripper? Very nice, too. I dunno how you manage to find 'em, Cass. And Mr Nobody at the end was a clever bit of casting. The real Tennel touch."

"They believe it, Drewy. They believe he's alive again."

"Good luck to 'em. But don't expect me to."

I felt the tiredness hit me like a hammer. I'd been holding back a tiny reserve of energy right through the programme, a little one-shot pistol for the battle with Patros. But he had disarmed and defeated me with a cynical chuckle and a totally unexpected word of praise. If he had attacked me I might have had a chance. As it was. . . .

I said, "Have there been any phone calls yet?"

"Four. Three during the programme. One just as you came off the air."

"What did they say?"

"The first three were a parson and two women, all complaining about the sequence in the cabaret. And the last one—" he chuckled again—"was a man asking for your belly-dancer's vital statistics."

I felt sick. All our preparation—the careful questions, Kapper's tight production, Greg's close-up shots—and all they could see was dirt.

"You still there, Cass?"

"Yes."

"When're you coming back?"

"Coming back? I don't know. Tomorrow, I suppose."

"You sound a bit frayed round the edges, boy. Been hectic, has it?"

"Mildly."

"Okay. Take a couple of days leave. Make it a week if you like. Fly up to the Lebanon and enjoy yourself for a change."

"Yes," I said. "I might do that."

"All right. I'll expect you back here a week from to-night. You and young Dekka. You can tell him I liked his work tonight, if you don't think it'll swell his head."

"I'll do that."

"Good. Is Nick Kapper still there?"

"Yes, I'll put him on, Er—Drewy?"

"Yes?"

"D'you think there'll be any reaction—after tonight, I mean? D'you think there'll be any trouble with. . . ?"

"Not a chance, Cass. Oh, we might get the odd crank writing in. But it'll only be cranks. Nobody in his right mind's going to take seriously the idea of a dead man walking about in Jerusalem."

"But I thought you were taking it seriously—yesterday morning when you rang up—I thought you said it could be dynamite."

"For God's sake, Cass, you've been working too hard or something. It could've been dynamite, politically speaking. But, as you've shewn us tonight, politically it's as dead as a dodo. Just a religious storm in a tea-cup. Could've been dull as hell with anyone but you handling it."

"Yes," I said. "I see."

"Off you go, Cass. A few days in the mountains with a little Lebanese play-mate and you'll be right as rain. Now, let me speak to Kapper."

I handed the phone to Nick and sat down heavily. My hands were shaking and my eyes burned and I felt as though I hadn't slept for a week. I wanted to weep, but I was too tired for tears, and too drained.

After a minute or two Kapper put the phone down and came and sat opposite me.

"I'm sorry, Cass."

I nodded. "I don't suppose we can blame him. He's not met them, any of them. He's only seen them in miniature on a black and white screen. It's not the same as talking to them face to face."

Through the window beside the console I could see Simon Cleopas sitting by the desk in the now deserted studio, with the bowl of flowers from Galilee in front of him. He looked small and lonely, incredibly nondescript now that the big lights were off.

I said, "Did Patros tell you about the phone calls?"

He nodded.

I kicked angrily at the console. "This damned box of tricks with its electronic eyes. You feed in a miracle and it comes out dirty."

"He also said he liked the programme, Cass."

"He wasn't supposed to like it, damn his smug little mind. He was supposed to believe it."

179

Kapper shook his head. "Not a chance, boy. Not our Drewy. If you'd put Davidson himself on camera, with a label tied round his neck and a set of finger-prints to prove it, you wouldn't have convinced Patros."

"Or the great viewing public sitting in front of their sets stuffing their greedy little bellies with fish and chips and sniggering over the spicy bits."

"A shade exaggerated, but you've got the right idea."

"Why?" I said. "What's the matter with them?"

He shrugged. "They don't want to believe it, Cass, any more than you do'"

"That's not true." I could hear the shrillness in my voice.

"Isn't it?" he said quietly.

Down in the studio Simon Cleopas was looking anxiously at his watch and glancing up at the window of the production-box.

"Poor little chap," Kapper said gently. "All mixed-up in something he doesn't understand." He looked at me, the rings of tiredness dark round his eyes. "They haven't got a hope you know, Cass. Even if Davidson has come back, they don't stand a chance."

"I think they do."

He shook his head. "No, Cass. You know they don't. You can't change the world—the great, greedy, frightened viewing public—with a handful of wise sayings, a seasoning of compassion and a miracle or two."

"Even if one of the miracles is a dead man come back to life?"

"Not even then. Especially not then. We're not ready for it, Cass. One day perhaps, when we're a little more intelligent, or a little more afraid of ourselves. But not yet. Not now."

He got up and held out his hand. "Come on, Cass. It's been a long day, Time we went home."

I said hopelessly, "But the world he promised them. The freedom and. . . ."

He smiled, a small, tired smile. "It's no use, Cass. We like it in prison. We don't want to be rescued."